THE ROYAL HOUSE OF KAREDES

Two crowns, two islands, one legacy

A royal family, torn apart by pride and its lust for power, reunited by purity and passion

The islands of Adamas ha~~ve~~ ~~been split~~ into
two ~~islands: Aristo~~ ~~and Calista~~

The ~~crowns~~

~~TWO ISL~~ANDS

Gorgeous Greek princes reign supreme
over glamorous Aristo
Smouldering sheikhs rule the desert island of Calista

ONE LEGACY
Whoever reunites the diamonds will rule all.

THE ROYAL HOUSE OF KAREDES

Many years ago there were two islands ruled as one kingdom – Adamas. But bitter family feuds and rivalry caused the kingdom to be ripped in two. The islands were ruled separately, as Aristo and Calista, and the infamous Stefani coronation diamond was split as a symbol of the feud and placed in the two new crowns.

But when the king divided the islands between his son and daughter, he left them with these words:

"You will rule each island for the good of the people and bring out the best in your kingdom. But my wish is that eventually these two jewels, like the islands, will be reunited. Aristo and Calista are more successful, more beautiful and more powerful as one nation: Adamas."

Now, King Aegeus Karedes of Aristo is dead, the island's coronation diamond is missing! The Aristans will stop at nothing to get it back but the ruthless sheikh king of Calista is hot on their heels.

Whether by seduction, blackmail or marriage, the jewel must be found. As the stories unfold, secrets and sins from the past are revealed and desire, love and passion war with royal duty. But who will discover in time that it is innocence of body and purity of heart that can unite the islands of Adamas once again?

THE ROYAL
HOUSE OF KAREDES

THE GREEK BILLIONAIRE'S
INNOCENT PRINCESS
CHANTELLE SHAW

Presented by

MILLS & BOON®
MODERN™

For my husband, Adrian,
with love and thanks for all your support.

First published in Great Britain 2009
by Harlequin Mills & Boon Limited,
Eton House, 18-24 Paradise Road, Richmond, Surrey TW9 1SR

The Greek Billionaire's Innocent Princess
© Harlequin Books S.A. 2009

Special thanks and acknowledgement are given to Chantelle Shaw
for her contribution to *The Royal House of Karedes* series

ISBN: 978 0 263 87556 0

53-0809

Printed and bound in Spain
by Litografia Rosés S.A., Barcelona

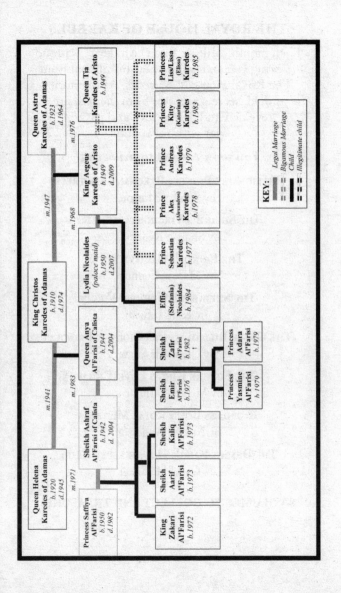

KEY:

- ———— Legal Marriage
- – – – – Bigamous Marriage
- ▬▬▬▬ Child
- ▪ ▪ ▪ ▪ Illegitimate child

Queen Helena Karedes of Adamas b.1920 d.1945

Queen Astra Karedes of Adamas b.1923 d.1964

King Christos Karedes of Adamas b.1910 d.1974

m.1941

m.1947

Queen Tia Karedes of Aristo b.1949

King Aegeus Karedes of Aristo b.1949 d.2009

m.1968

m.1976

Lydia Nicolaides (palace maid) b.1950 d.2007

Queen Anya Al'Farisi of Calista b.1944 d.2004

Sheikh Ashraf Al'Farisi of Calista b.1942 d.2004

m.1983

Princess Saffiya Al'Farisi b.1950 d.1982

m.1971

Princess Liss/Lissa (Elissa) Karedes b.1985

Princess Kitty (Katarina) Karedes b.1983

Prince Andreas Karedes b.1979

Prince Alex (Alexandros) Karedes b.1978

Prince Sebastian Karedes b.1977

Effie (Stefania) Nicolaides b.1984

Sheikh Zaffir Al'Farisi b.1982

Sheikh Emir Al'Farisi b.1976

Sheikh Kaliq Al'Farisi b.1973

Sheikh Aarif Al'Farisi b.1973

King Zakari Al'Farisi b.1972

Princess Adara Al'Farisi b.1979

Princess Yasmine Al'Farisi b.1970

THE ROYAL HOUSE OF KAREDES

Each month, Mills & Boon® Modern™ is proud
to bring you an exciting new instalment from
The Royal House of Karedes. As the stories
unfold, secrets and sins from the past are
revealed and desire, love and passion
war with royal duty!

You won't want to miss out!

BILLIONAIRE PRINCE, PREGNANT MISTRESS
by Sandra Marton

THE SHEIKH'S VIRGIN STABLE-GIRL
by Sharon Kendrick

THE PRINCE'S CAPTIVE WIFE
by Marion Lennox

THE SHEIKH'S FORBIDDEN VIRGIN
by Kate Hewitt

THE GREEK BILLIONAIRE'S INNOCENT PRINCESS
by Chantelle Shaw

THE FUTURE KING'S LOVE-CHILD
by Melanie Milburne

RUTHLESS BOSS, ROYAL MISTRESS
by Natalie Anderson

THE DESERT KING'S HOUSEKEEPER BRIDE
by Carol Marinelli

8 VOLUMES TO COLLECT AND TREASURE!

CHAPTER ONE

NIKOS ANGELAKI stood at the edge of the ballroom and surveyed the five hundred or so guests who were dancing or sipping champagne beneath the ornate chandeliers. The men were uniform in black tuxedos, while the women—dressed in couture gowns and flaunting a spectacular array of diamonds and precious gems—flitted about the dance floor like gaudy butterflies. He flicked back the cuff of his dinner jacket, glanced at his Rolex, and then began to make his way across the room—aware of the interested glances he received as he passed. At thirty-two he was used to the attention his looks and the rumours of his wealth attracted. An attractive blonde in a daringly low-cut dress caught his attention, and his gaze lingered on her fleetingly before he stepped into the lobby.

It was the first time he had attended the royal ball or visited the Aristan palace, and he was impressed by the elegant splendour of the rooms where the silk-covered walls were lined with priceless works of art. The ruling family of the House of Karedes was one of the wealthiest families in Europe, and the guest-list included members of the aristocracy and heads of state— grand people who had no idea that the Prince Regent's honoured guest tonight had grown up in the slums of Athens.

Nikos wondered cynically if the butler who had escorted him to the state drawing room to greet Prince Sebastian would have been quite so obsequious if he'd known that Nikos's mother had once worked as a lowly kitchen maid at the palace. However, that was something he hadn't even revealed to Sebastian, despite the close friendship that had developed between them.

He strode across the hall, pushed open a door, and found himself in the banqueting suite, which was empty, apart from a waitress at the far end of the room who—unlike the other palace staff who seemed to be rushed off their feet tonight—was idly folding napkins.

The guests had eaten earlier, but Nikos's delayed flight had meant that he had missed the buffet supper, and as he glanced at the mouth-watering selection of canapés he was aware of a hollow feeling in his stomach. Business first, he told himself firmly. It was evening in Aristo, but early afternoon on America's east coast and he had arranged to call a client in New York. He strolled towards the waitress who had her back to him and was still oblivious to his presence.

'Can you tell me if there is somewhere I can be uninterrupted? I need to make an urgent business call.'

The deep, gravelly voice was so innately sensual that the tiny hairs on Kitty's body stood on end, and she turned her head, her heart crashing in her chest when she stared up at the man who had come silently into the room. She had recognised him instantly when he had walked into the ballroom earlier in the evening—Nikos Angelaki, billionaire shipping magnate, notorious playboy, and in recent months one of her brother's closest confidants. Sebastian had explained that he had met Nikos at a business function in Greece, and since then the two men had discovered a mutual liking for poker and the roulette wheel in the nightclubs of Aristo and Athens.

The photographs Kitty had seen of him in the tabloids had triggered her interest, but nothing had prepared her for the impact of Nikos in the flesh. He was suave, sophisticated and spine-tinglingly sexy. Taller than average; his tapered black trousers emphasised his long legs and taut thighs, while his impeccably tailored dinner jacket cloaked formidably broad shoulders. But it was his face that captured her attention. Handsome was a barely adequate description of the chiselled perfection of his features: the slanting, razor-sharp cheekbones and square chin, the heavy brows arched above midnight-dark eyes, and a wide, sensual mouth.

In the silence that stretched between them Kitty sensed his arrogance and devil-may-care confidence, and she felt an unbidden and shockingly intense tug of sexual awareness that sent a quiver down her spine. He was gorgeous, but she suddenly realised that she was staring at him, and she blushed.

'There is a small sitting room through there,' she mumbled, indicating the door at the far end of the room.

'Thank you.'

His eyes skimmed over her, making a brief inspection of her unexciting black cocktail dress, and Kitty wished fervently that she had bought a new outfit for the ball—something slinky and low-cut that would have made him look at her with male appreciation, rather than dismiss her without a second glance.

But she had never been very interested in clothes, preferring her research work for Aristo's museum to shopping, and it had only been when she had flicked through her list of preparations for the ball and seen the words 'buy dress' that she'd realised she had nothing suitable to wear to the palace's most prestigious social event.

She lacked the confidence to wear sexy outfits, anyway, she acknowledged dismally. And she certainly wouldn't stand a chance with a man like Nikos. He had given no sign that he recognised her, but palace protocol dictated that she should make the first introduction. Immediately she felt tongue-tied by the crippling shyness that had afflicted her since childhood. Not for the first time she wished she shared her sister Princess Elissa's self-confidence and sparkling personality. Liss always made socialising look so easy.

She was Princess Katarina Karedes, fourth in line to the throne of Aristo, Kitty reminded herself. She had been trained practically from birth to deal with social situations, but she had never found meeting new people easy, and she was still steeling herself to offer her hand to Nikos in formal greeting when he spoke again.

'I've a feeling that you are needed to serve champagne in the ballroom. I understand from Prince Sebastian that a number of the catering staff have been taken ill, and I noticed that many of the guests have empty glasses.' He gave her a faint, dismissive smile, as if he expected her to immediately scuttle off, and turned his attention to his phone.

Kitty gaped at him, overwhelmed by his powerful personality, and taken aback by his suggestion that she was needed to serve drinks. She was aware of the problem with the caterers she had booked to work alongside the palace staff, and, having spent the past month planning every detail of the ball like a military operation, she found it annoying that so many of the waiters had succumbed to a virulent sickness virus. Anxious to ensure that the evening ran smoothly she had come to the banqueting room to check over the buffet table, but the head butler had assured her that everything was under control, and she was sure it was not necessary for her to take on the role of waitress.

Usually she had little to do with the royal ball, but this year, with Queen Tia mourning the death of the king, Sebastian had asked her to oversee the arrangements. Seb had enough on his mind, Kitty thought ruefully. After their father's unexpected death Sebastian should have immediately become the new king. But the shocking discovery that the Aristan half of the Stefani diamond, which was set in the Aristan Crown, was a fake, and that the real diamond was missing, had thrown the plans for his coronation into disarray. By royal tradition Sebastian could not be crowned if he did not have the jewel, and until it was found he could only assume the title of Prince Regent.

Lost in her thoughts, Kitty suddenly realised that Nikos Angelaki was watching her with unconcealed impatience. He moved away and began to punch numbers into his phone. 'My client is expecting my call,' he said as he walked towards the door leading to the sitting room. 'And you had better get back to work.' He paused, and looked back at her. 'Actually, you could bring me some champagne—and while you're about it something from the buffet. The *dolmathakia* looks good, and perhaps some bread and olives.'

He was a guest, Kitty reminded herself, and her duty as hostess of the ball was to ensure that the guests enjoyed the evening. But his haughty tone rankled. It was usual for people she did not know to address her as Your Highness, but Nikos was either unaware or unimpressed that he should use her royal title. Throughout her life Kitty had been treated with a deference suited to her royal status. She did not expect to be fawned over, but Nikos had spoken to her as if she were a lackey. Didn't he know who she was?

'You want *me* to serve you?' she queried, taken aback by his arrogant demand.

Her sharp tone caught Nikos's attention and he glanced across the room, his eyes narrowing when he noted the waitress's mutinous expression. He had paid scant attention to her when he had first walked into the room, and had formed a vague impression of a dumpy, rather plain girl in a badly fitting dress. But now, as he studied her more closely, he realised that she was far from uninteresting.

She was unfashionably curvaceous, he mused idly, allowing his gaze to roam over the swell of her hips that flared below her neat waist. Her voluptuous breasts straining beneath her dress would make a generous handful. A vivid mental picture came into his mind of her wearing a strapless, low-cut couture gown that displayed her breasts like plump, round peaches. In his imagination he saw himself slowly removing the gown, drawing it down and feasting his eyes on her nakedness, and he felt his body tighten with unbidden sexual awareness.

She wasn't his type, he reminded himself irritably. He liked tall, elegant blondes, and she was a short, curvy brunette. Her heavy-rimmed glasses were unflattering, but he noted that her skin was smooth and tinted a pale olive-gold, her slanting cheekbones highlighted by a flush of rose-pink, and her mouth was wide, her lips full and lush and eminently kissable.

Hell! He'd obviously been celibate for too long, he thought sardonically. He was a self-confessed workaholic, and under his leadership Petridis Angelaki Shipping's profits had soared. He worked hard and played hard, but recently he hadn't played enough. It was time he redressed the balance—but he doubted Prince Sebastian would be pleased if he seduced a member of the palace staff.

'If it's not too much trouble,' he drawled sarcastically. 'It is your job, after all.'

Kitty thought of the hours she'd spent organising the party, and felt a spurt of temper. She'd been run ragged for weeks, anxious to ensure the ball was a success for Sebastian's sake, but her duties didn't include acting as a personal attendant to one of her brother's friends. Twin spots of colour burned on her cheeks, and she put her hands on her hips.

'The idea of the buffet table is that guests can help themselves,' she informed Nikos tightly.

She saw him frown as his eyes trailed over her, and it suddenly struck her that her high-necked, long-sleeved black dress—which she had bought two seasons ago in the hope that the starkly simple style would make her look slimmer—was almost identical to the uniform that the female serving staff were wearing. *Her job!* Understanding slowly dawned. Could it be that Nikos Angelaki had no idea of her identity? They had never met, and, unlike Liss, who was often pictured in the tabloids, she was rarely recognised by the paparazzi. Nikos clearly believed she was one of the palace staff, and she didn't know whether to be amused or insulted by the mistake.

She opened her mouth to tell him that she was Princess Katarina, not a lowly servant, but something held her back. It was humiliating that he had mistaken her for a waitress. She wished now that she had made more effort with her appearance instead of blithely assuming that no one would take much notice of her. She was acting as the Prince Regent's consort tonight, and people *had* noticed her, but for all the wrong reasons.

During the evening she had overheard various unflattering comments from the guests that she was the Plain Jane Princess who had missed out on her sister's looks: *'…twenty-six…oh, no, not married…must be hard to be in the shadow of lovely Liss. Apparently Princess Katarina is the brainy one, but she doesn't share Princess Elissa's beauty.'*

Kitty wondered how Nikos would react when she told him she was a princess. Would he share the general consensus of the guests that she was the ugly duckling of the family? It didn't help that he was so stunningly good-looking. She could feel her heart thudding erratically as she absorbed the masculine beauty of his face, and she was startled by a fierce longing to run her fingers through the lock of silky black hair that had fallen forwards onto his brow.

She was terrified that he could somehow read her mind, but she could not tear her eyes from his, and she sensed something indefinable pass between them that made her skin prickle and her breasts tingle. To her horror she felt her nipples swell beneath her dress and she hastily crossed her arms over her chest, her cheeks burning.

Nikos recognised the flare of sexual awareness in the waitress's eyes and was infuriated by his own body's involuntary reaction to it. He did not have time to waste dealing with a stroppy domestic, even though the chemistry between them was tangible. 'I suggest you look up the word "servant",' he said coldly. 'You'll find it means "someone who is paid to serve". I'm sure Prince Sebastian is a fair employer who pays you a generous wage, and I would be grateful if you could do as I've asked without further argument.'

He should walk through into the private sitting room and make his call—but for reasons he couldn't explain, he hesitated. He could not dismiss the ridiculous urge to pull the girl into his arms and kiss her senseless. Not a girl, he corrected himself, his eyes drawn once again to the firm swell of her breasts. She was very much a woman, with a gorgeous hourglass figure that might not be 'in' with the fashion police but was incredibly sexy. He felt a fierce tug of sexual hunger in his groin and inhaled sharply, his nostrils flaring. 'What is your name?' he demanded harshly.

'It's…Rina.' The words spilled from Kitty's lips, and the moment they were out it was too late to retract them. She didn't understand what had prompted her to withhold her true identity, but she knew that Nikos had previously met Liss at a party in Paris and, although it was stupid, she could not bear the idea of him comparing her with her beautiful, glamorous sister. 'I'm new here,' she mumbled, assuring herself that she had only lied to save him the embarrassment of learning that he had mistaken a member of the royal family for a servant.

'I see.' Nikos strolled back across the room towards her and Kitty felt her pulse-rate quicken with every step he took. He swamped her senses and she was tempted to turn and flee, but when he halted inches from her she saw the gleam of sexual curiosity in his eyes and shock held her immobile. Surely she was wrong? Nikos had dated some of the world's most beautiful women and it was rumoured that he had been having a white-hot affair with the stunning Hollywood star, Shannon Marsh, for months. It was inconceivable that he could be attracted to a frump like her—wasn't it? She licked her suddenly dry lips and was startled when the expression in his eyes hardened to a predatory gleam that caused her heart to pound.

'Something tells me you have a lot to learn, Rina.'

The mockery in his voice was mixed with a blatant sensual message that sent a quiver of excitement down Kitty's spine. She had led a sheltered life at the palace, and at twenty-six was painfully aware of her sexual inexperience, but the feral heat in Nikos's eyes was unmistakable, even to a novice like her.

'I'd better go…and bring you some champagne, Mr Angelaki,' she said breathlessly, jerking away from him before she gave in to the temptation to close the space between them and press her soft body against the muscled hardness of his. Dangerous thoughts; and instinct warned her he was a man who was way out of her league.

'Yes, you better had.' Nikos laughed softly, self-derisively; breaking the web of sexual tension that curvy little waitress had somehow woven around him. 'Out of interest, how do you know my name?'

'I've seen your photograph, and read about you in the newspapers,' Kitty admitted, although she did not add that she regularly scanned the tabloids for articles about him or that she was rarely disappointed by his absence in the gossip columns. Nikos Angelaki's luck at the roulette table was as legendary as his business acumen. He was a gambler and a risk-taker, a high-flier who was frequently snapped by the paparazzi driving around Athens in his Lamborghini with a seemingly inexhaustible supply of beautiful women at his side. 'You have a reputation as a millionaire playboy with a different blonde on your arm almost every week,' she said stiffly.

Nikos shrugged carelessly. 'You shouldn't believe all you read in the papers, Rina. Some of my "blondes" have lasted much longer than a week, and a few have even made it to a month,' he added sardonically. 'But I think my private life is nobody's business but my own—don't you?'

'Absolutely,' Kitty replied tightly, stung by his rebuke. 'It's no concern of mine that you change your women as often as other men change their socks.'

An ominous pause followed her defiant statement, and then Nikos threw back his head and laughed. 'I wonder if Prince Sebastian is aware that he has a rebel among his staff?' he drawled, moving before Kitty had time to react, and capturing her chin between his strong fingers. 'If you're not careful that sassy mouth could get you into a lot of trouble, Rina.'

She was trapped by his closeness, and the heat from his body mingled with the sensual tang of his aftershave stole around her and held her prisoner. The gleam in his eyes sent a tremor through her, and for a few electrifying seconds she thought he was going to lower his head and kiss her. She held her breath, torn between fear and fascination, and felt a crushing sense of disappointment when he abruptly released her. Of course he hadn't intended to kiss her; stupid of her to have thought it.

Nikos wondered if she knew how easily he

could read her mind—or how tempted he was to accept her unspoken invitation and crush her soft mouth beneath his. It took every ounce of his will power to step away from her and retrace his steps back across the room. 'Go back to the ballroom before I decide to tell the prince of your reluctance to do the job you are employed to do,' he said tersely. 'And, Rina—' he paused in the doorway of the sitting room '—don't forget my champagne, will you?'

His arrogance was breathtaking. It was on Kitty's lips to tell him that under Aristo's ancient laws his lack of respect for a member of the royal family was a serious offence. He was lucky she did not call for the palace guard, and have him thrown out, she thought angrily. She was renowned for her calm and peaceable nature, but she was infuriated by his insolence.

But it was her own idiotic fault that he believed she was a waitress, and, uttering a most unprincesslike curse, she swung on her heels and marched out of the banqueting hall.

CHAPTER TWO

KITTY spent the rest of the evening carefully avoiding Nikos Angelaki, but she could not forget him, or the electricity that had fizzed between them when they had been alone together. No man had ever looked at her the way Nikos had done—with a raw, sexual hunger in his eyes that had evoked a wild longing deep inside her and left her wishing that he had swept her into his arms and made passionate love to her on the banqueting table.

Unable to dismiss her shocking fantasy from her mind, she had been too embarrassed to face him again with the food and champagne he had requested, and had asked one of the staff to serve him. Later, she had hovered behind a pillar, and watched him partner a steady stream of beautiful women on the dance floor. If it hadn't been for her stupid lie she could have asked Sebastian to introduce them, and maybe he would have asked her to dance. But if she revealed her identity to him now she would look a complete idiot in front of Nikos, and her brother.

She wouldn't know what to say to him anyway, she acknowledged bleakly. She was hopeless with men. The few fledgling romances she'd had at university had been disastrous and she knew her family despaired of her ever finding a husband. Kitty sighed, weighted down by the familiar feeling that she was a failure. Her dress was uncomfortably tight and tendrils of her hair had come loose and curled about her hot face. She wished the ball were over. She'd spent so long fretting over it and she was glad it was a success but she longed for the quiet solitude of the palace library and her books.

The king had shared her fascination with the history of the Adamas Kingdom, and she treasured her memories of the evenings they had spent together researching their ancestors. Nothing was the same without her father, she thought bleakly. One day soon Sebastian would be crowned King and she would give him her full support, but she missed King Aegeus desperately.

Grief surged through her and she bit her lip, knowing that she must control it as Queen Tia managed to do when she was in public. She was tired of the party, and she stepped through the French doors leading onto the terrace. The night air was warm and heavy with the perfume of jasmine and honeysuckle, and the silence was blissful after the hubbub of voices in the ballroom, but her peace did not last long.

'Well, well. Kitty Karedes! I didn't realise it was you. I saw a woman slip furtively out of the ballroom, and assumed she was meeting a lover, but, unless the ice-princess has thawed considerably since we last met, that's not likely, is it?'

'Vasilis! I won't lie and say it's a pleasure to see you. But the idea of you sneaking out to spy on lovers is wholly believable,' Kitty replied contemptuously. She glanced at Vasilis Sarondakos, felt the familiar wave of revulsion sweep over her and turned her back on him, hoping he would get the message and leave her alone. But Vasilis was not renowned for his sensitivity.

The Sarondakos family were leading members of Aristo's aristocracy, and Vasilis's father, Constantine, had been a close friend of the late king. At eighteen, Kitty had been painfully naïve, and had never had a boyfriend. With her father's encouragement she had gone on a date with Vasilis, but she had been deeply traumatised when he had subjected her to a drunken assault. His taunts that her voluptuous body was designed for sex had been devastating, but she had been too ashamed to tell her family what had happened, believing Vasilis's assertion that because she had worn a low-cut dress she had been—in his words—'gagging for it'.

The memory of his hot, alcohol-fuelled breath on her skin and his sweaty hands tearing her dress and touching her breasts still haunted her, and when her father had suggested a couple of years ago that he would be pleased if she married the son of his dear friend, Constantine Sarondakos, he had been taken aback by her fierce refusal.

'So, still no sign of a husband on the horizon, then, Kitty?' Vasilis taunted, coming to stand so close to her that she found herself trapped between him and the low stone wall that encircled the terrace. 'You should have married me while you had the chance.'

'I'd sooner swallow poison.' Kitty tried to edge away from him and tension knotted her stomach when he leaned closer still and rested his hands on the wall on either side of her, effectively caging her in. Five hundred guests were packed into the ballroom less than six feet away, including her three overprotective brothers. She had nothing to fear from Vasilis but she detested his cocky smile and the way he was looking at her as if he was mentally undressing her.

'Is that so?' Vasilis gave a sneering laugh. 'Perhaps you shouldn't be so hasty, my prim little princess. I was talking to Sebastian just the other day and he confided his concern that you'll end up on the shelf; a lonely spinster with only her books for company.'

'I'm twenty-six, not ninety-six,' Kitty snapped. 'And I don't believe for a minute that Sebastian would discuss my private affairs with you.'

'He'd have great difficulty; you don't have affairs.' Vasilis laughed again, clearly proud of his wit. 'I bet you're still a virgin, aren't you, Kitty? Of course, a lot of people think you're a lesbian,' he added conversationally. 'Maybe that's why Sebastian would like to see you married. With rumours that the Stefani diamond is a fake, and Sebastian delaying his coronation, the gossip is that your Calistan cousin Zakari is laying claim to the throne. The people of Aristo are already unsettled. The Karedes family don't need another scandal.'

'There is no scandal! Sebastian *is* the rightful king and he will be crowned as soon as possible,' Kitty said fiercely. 'Zakari Al'Farisi is the King of Calista but he has no right to Aristo's crown, or to be the one ruler of the Adamas Islands.' Kitty wasn't sure how Vasilis had heard the news the diamond was a fake, but she certainly wasn't going to confirm the rumour. 'The people of Aristo have nothing to worry about.

'As for me ever marrying you—hell will freeze over first!' Using all her strength, she pushed against Vasilis's arm until she broke free. 'Leave me alone, Vasilis. You sicken me. I never told my family about what happened between us out of respect for the affection my father felt for yours. But now Papa is dead and if you ever come near me again I'll tell my brothers what kind of a man you are, and you will no longer be welcome at the palace.'

'It'll be your word against mine,' Vasilis muttered, but his bravado was short-lived. The Karedeses were a tight-knit family who he knew would close ranks around one of their own. 'Anyway, do you really think I'd want to marry a woman who's as sexually responsive as a lump of ice?' he demanded spitefully. 'You've got some serious hang-ups about sex, Kitty. Maybe you should see a therapist.'

'I don't have any hang-ups…' Kitty ground her teeth in impotent fury as Vasilis grinned and sauntered through the French doors. She stared after him, knowing she should return to the ballroom, but simply unable to face it. Vasilis's cruel jibes played over and over in her head, compounding her misery that she was a hopeless failure.

She was a princess and she was supposed to be beautiful and glamorous. She was supposed to sparkle at social events and impress everyone with her sophistication and wit, but instead of being the belle of the royal ball tonight she had been mistaken for a waitress. She had never been any good at the whole royal thing, she thought drearily—the pomp and ceremony and waving at crowds—and it had been easier to leave the socialising that was a necessary part of royal life to Liss, and bury herself in the library with her books.

Was that going to be her life? she wondered desperately. Was she going to end up a spinster as Vasilis had prophesied—without love or passion, clinging to the memories of the night a gorgeous, sexy Greek tycoon had almost kissed her? Tears blurred her eyes and misted her glasses, and the sound of music and laughter from the ballroom made her feel lonelier than ever.

With a choked cry she raced down the terrace steps, away from the ballroom, and flew across the lawn. Tonight, when she'd stood at the edge of the ballroom and noted how everyone else seemed to be part of a couple she had faced the fact that she was a lonely, virgin princess, stifled by the formality of royal life. Her brothers and sister seemed to be moving on, but she felt as though she were trapped in a time warp. She had been born at the palace and had always loved it, but suddenly it felt like a prison and she was desperate to be free—to escape a life of duty and find out who Kitty Karedes really was.

She ran through the formal gardens, away from the lights spilling from the ballroom. The perimeter wall of the palace grounds was ten feet tall and built of impenetrable stone, but Kitty knew of the secret gate, half overgrown with climbing roses. In the moonlight she easily found the loose brick in the wall, and the hidden key, and seconds later she fled down a narrow path that led into a small cave at the base of the cliff.

Blow Vasilis Sarondakos and his spiteful tongue! she thought as she scrubbed her eyes. She wasn't on the shelf; she didn't have hang-ups about sex, and so what if she was still a virgin at twenty-six? It didn't make her less of a woman! She kicked her shoes off and wandered down to the water's edge, soothed by the gentle lap of the waves on the shore. She knew she would not be disturbed here. This little cove was a private beach, and the only way to it was along the path from the palace—a path that few people outside the family knew about.

Moonlight dappled the sea so that it shimmered like a flat silver pool. No one could see her here. She was completely alone, and impulsively she wrenched open the buttons on the hateful black dress and tugged it down over her hips until it dropped onto the sand. She placed her glasses carefully on a rock and pulled the pins from her hair, shaking her head so that her glossy dark chestnut tresses uncoiled and fell almost to her waist.

With each item of clothing she removed she felt as though she were discarding another hurtful jibe. So what if she didn't have a model-thin figure? Women were meant to have breasts, and she wasn't ashamed of hers. The silver sea beckoned her; she was already relishing the coolness of it on her skin, and in a moment of defiance against the restrictions of her life she unsnapped her bra, dropped it on top of her dress and stepped out of her knickers before running naked into the water with her hair streaming behind her.

Nikos was not sorry that the royal ball was drawing to an end. He had flown to Aristo from Dubai after a week of intense negotiations, and the eighteen-hour days he'd spent in the board-room were catching up with him. He liked and admired Prince Sebastian, but he was bored of the other guests' endless, inane chit-chat, the gossip about who was sleeping with whom, and the unsubtle hints from a number of women that they were willing to go to bed with him.

Maybe he was simply tired of blondes, he mused as he stepped out onto the terrace, a half-full bottle of champagne in one hand and his dinner jacket looped over his shoulder. All evening he had been frustrated by his inability to dismiss the waitress, Rina, from his mind. He hadn't seen her again after their confrontation in the banqueting hall but he knew he hadn't imagined the chemistry between them. She intrigued him more than any woman had done for a long time, and he had found himself scanning the ballroom for her, irritated by his disappointment that she seemed to have disappeared.

He strolled through the shadowy gardens. The palace was as amazing as his mother had led him to believe many years ago when she had recounted tales of the time she had worked here before he had been born. As a child he had listened in awe to her description of the huge rooms and opulent décor, and as he'd looked around the cramped, run-down apartment block where they had lived it had seemed impossible that such a grand place existed.

He walked to the far end of the garden and was about to turn back when he recalled a distant memory his mother had told him of a gate in the wall, and a path that led from the palace to the beach. With a faint, self-derisive smile on his lips at his curiosity Nikos took one of the Chinese lanterns that illuminated the path and held it aloft as he walked back to the wall. The gate was tucked into a corner, and well disguised by the rose bushes that grew around it. He pushed it, expecting it to be locked, but when it opened he was sufficiently intrigued to follow the path that led from it.

The ground sloped steeply down until it disappeared between an opening in the rocks. Nikos had to duck his head as he entered the cave. It was dry inside, he noted, when he swung the lantern from side to side. Obviously the tide never came up this far. The air smelled faintly of seaweed and through the cave he could see the sea shimmering silver in the moonlight, but as he emerged onto the beach he stopped abruptly, and his heart kicked in his chest. For a moment he wondered if his mind was playing tricks on him, but the woman standing a few feet away from him was undoubtedly real, and her hourglass figure was instantly recognisable—even without her clothes.

Kitty swam right across the bay and back again with clean, strong strokes and then flipped onto her back and stared up at the moon, and the crystal stars that studded the midnight sky. She felt bold and empowered—as unashamedly naked as Eve had been in the Garden of Eden. There was something wickedly sensuous about the silken slide of the water over her bare limbs. She loved swimming and in the water she felt as light and graceful as a water nymph—at peace with her body instead of hating it for not conforming to the model slender form she had tried, through numerous diets and exercise regimes, to acquire.

Vasilis wouldn't be so ready to taunt her about her supposed sexual hang-ups if he could see her now, she thought as she turned onto her front and allowed the waves to carry her back to the shore. The beach was shadowed and mysterious in the moonlight. The huge boulders that stood guard at either end of the cove loomed like faceless giants, but despite the darkness and her short-sightedness Kitty could distinctly make out the figure of a man, and her heart almost leapt from her chest.

Dear God! Had Vasilis followed her? Fear uncoiled in the pit of her stomach, a wave caught her unawares and dragged her under, and she bobbed back to the surface gagging from the salt water she'd swallowed but desperate not to cough and attract the attention of the intruder. It had to be Vasilis. Few of the other guests at the ball were aware of the path leading from the palace to the beach, but Vasilis knew about it and had come here several times with her brothers.

The prospect of meeting her tormentor on the secluded beach sent a shiver of trepidation down Kitty's spine. She had seen the way he'd looked at her on the terrace, his lecherous grin that had changed to anger when she'd made it clear that she wanted nothing to do with him. Vasilis would not have dared lay a finger on her outside the ballroom, but here there was no one to help her— or hear her scream.

Clouds drifted across the moon, blotting out its brilliant gleam and plunging the beach into pitch blackness, and, seizing her chance, Kitty tore up the sand and crouched behind a rock. Her breath came in shallow gasps and her heart was pounding when the figure strolled down towards the water's edge.

'Hello, Rina,' he drawled. 'This is the second time tonight I've caught you playing hooky. Shouldn't you be busy at work at the ball?'

For a few seconds shock rendered Kitty speechless. *'You!'* she spluttered at last as the clouds above them parted and moonlight danced across Nikos Angelaki's sculpted features. Attack seemed the best form of defence and although her nakedness forced her to remain behind the rock her voice was sharp when she snapped, 'Do you know you're trespassing? This is a private beach.'

'Indeed it is. It belongs to the royal family, and I have express permission from Prince Sebastian to be here,' Nikos replied coolly. 'The only trespasser is you—unless the prince has suddenly opened up the beach for use by the palace staff. Do you have permission to be here, Rina?'

Kitty stared at him wordlessly, not knowing how to answer without revealing her true identity. She was agonisingly aware that she was naked, and she wished a hole would appear at her feet and swallow her up. 'The party hasn't finished yet. What are you doing here?' she mumbled in a voice thick with embarrassment.

In the pearly light cast by the moon she saw Nikos shrug. 'It was hot in the ballroom, and I decided to walk down to the beach for some fresh air. I could hardly believe my eyes when I came through the cave and caught sight of you.'

'You should have said something. I believed I was alone,' Kitty said miserably, burning up with mortification when she recalled how she had stripped out of her clothes. She prayed Nikos had arrived after she had run into the sea, but he swiftly shattered her tenuous hope.

'I was afraid I'd startle you,' he drawled. His voice dipped and the amusement in his tone was mixed with something else. 'Besides, what red-blooded male would have spoken out and risked spoiling the show? I was so careful not to make a sound that I barely drew breath.' He paused for a heartbeat and then said quietly, 'Watching you slowly reveal your body was the most erotic ex-perience I've ever had.'

In a corner of her mind Kitty registered that the teasing note had disappeared from his voice, and the undisguised sensuality in his deep tone sent a quiver of reaction down her spine. But the idea that she had unwittingly revealed her curvy figure, which she so despised, to him, made her want to weep with shame. 'You are disgusting!' she choked. 'I can just about swallow the line that you didn't want to scare me, but if you were a gentle-man you'd have shut your eyes.'

Nikos's rich laughter swirled around the empty

beach. 'Ah, but I have never professed to be a gentleman, Rina. I am a pirate, an opportunist who answers to no one, and I do what I please.' His voice lowered to a sexy growl, 'And I promise you, *agape,* you pleased me very much.'

Kitty did not know how to react to that startling statement, and she hugged her arms around herself and peeped warily over the top of the rock.

She was as tempting as a siren from Greek mythology, Nikos owned as he stared at bare shoulders and her mass of dark hair that fell in damp tendrils down her back. But he was not about to admit that he'd been so turned on when he had watched her remove her clothes that he'd almost embarrassed himself.

When he had first seen her, he had assumed that she must have come down to the beach for an assignation with a lover. But no one else had appeared, and if he was honest he'd been so stunned by the sight of her stepping out of her dress and running down to the sea that he had been struck dumb.

Before his eyes Rina had emerged from her cocoon of drab clothes, and he had been riveted by her beauty. Pale fingers of moonlight had illuminated every dip and curve of her body, and tinted her satiny skin with silver brushstrokes. He had held his breath when she'd released her hair and it had tumbled down her back like a river of pure silk, and exhaled sharply when she had un-fastened her bra and bared the creamy mounds of her full breasts to his hungry gaze.

His arousal had been instant and uncomfortably hard and his urgency to pillow himself between her soft thighs was still so acute that he was glad of the all concealing dark. It didn't seem to matter how much he tried to rationalise his reaction to her or remind himself that he liked slim, graceful blondes—and preferably the comfort of a large bed when he made love.

Rina had intrigued him in the banqueting hall earlier, when he had recognised the sizzling chemistry between them. Now, he desired her with a stark, primitive hunger that sent his blood thundering through his veins. He wanted to make love to her here on the sand, beneath the stars, and with a passion that was as wild and elemental as the untamed beach.

CHAPTER THREE

DESPITE the warmth of the night air Kitty was shivering—as much from the shock of Nikos's sudden appearance on the beach as from her swim. Her hair was hanging in wet coils and her skin was covered in goose-bumps but she reassured herself that her nipples had hardened into tight, tingling peaks because she was cold, *not* because of her overwhelming awareness of the sexiest man she had ever met.

She gritted her teeth to prevent them from chattering, and wished he would go back to the palace. Her dress was somewhere on the other side of the beach, but she would rather stay behind her rock all night and risk hypothermia than parade naked in front of him. She had already done so once, she acknowledged, blushing furiously again at the memory, but she had been unaware of his presence in the cave. No way was she going to make an exhibition of herself again.

'Here, put this on while I go and find your clothes.' Nikos stepped closer and dropped his jacket over the rock, and Kitty seized it gratefully and slipped it on. It was immense on her; the arms were several inches too long and to her relief the hem of the jacket reached to her mid-thighs. The silk lining felt deliciously sensuous against her skin; still warm from the heat of Nikos's body and carrying the faint musk of his aftershave. She burrowed deeper into the folds and inhaled deeply. She had been short-sighted for most of her life, but, as if to compensate for her poor vision, her other senses were particularly acute and she could detect his clean, male scent.

Molten heat stole through her veins as she imagined him wrapping his arms around her rather than his jacket. She remembered the fantasy she'd had earlier of him making love to her on the banqueting table, and pictured with shocking clarity him stripping out of his own clothes and tumbling her down on the sand. What was the matter with her? Scarlet-cheeked, she lifted her eyes to his, and caught her breath at the flash of fire she glimpsed before his lashes fell and hid his expression. But she had seen the desire in his gaze, and despite her inexperience she had recognised his need and found that it evoked an answering ache inside her.

She shivered again, and this time her whole

body trembled—with reaction to Nikos rather than cold. She saw him tense, saw his eyes narrow, and knew that the wildfire awareness between them was terrifyingly real. Incredible though it seemed, Nikos Angelaki—playboy and serial womaniser—found her attractive. For the first time ever in her twenty-six years she felt as though she was a desirable woman, and she wanted to savour the moment—certain that any second now he would blink and realise that she was too short, too plump and too plain to hold his attention for long.

'You had better wait in the cave, you'll be warmer there,' he said, suddenly breaking the silence. His voice sounded so harsh that Kitty wondered what had angered him. He turned and strode away, and Kitty hesitated, her heart hammering, before she stepped from behind her rock and hurried up the beach. Almost instantly he reappeared at her side and caught hold of her arm to swing her round to him. 'I assume you need these,' he murmured as he unfolded her glasses and placed them on her nose.

'Thank you.' Kitty stared transfixed at his features, which were now sharply defined rather than blurred. Moonbeams highlighted the angles and planes of his incredible bone-structure, and she could not tear her eyes from the firm line of his mouth.

She heard him draw a sharp breath, and she gasped when he slid his hand beneath her chin and tilted her face to his. 'Hasn't anyone ever told you it's dangerous to swim in the sea alone?' he demanded impatiently. 'You could have got into trouble in the current, and no one would have known.' His eyes dropped to her small frame enveloped by his jacket, and he tried unsuccessfully to dismiss the image of her running naked across the sand. 'Tell me, do you often swim naked in the moonlight?'

'No, of course not,' Kitty replied quickly, squirming. It was not entirely the truth, she acknowledged silently. She loathed the sight of her body in a bikini and often came to swim alone in the dark when no one would see her. 'I know this is a private beach, and I thought I would be undisturbed here,' she said pointedly. 'Like you, I came down for some fresh air, but the sea looked so inviting that I was overcome with a mad impulse to…strip off and dive in.'

'Is that so?' Nikos's voice was no longer harsh, but velvet soft, stroking over Kitty's skin so that each tiny hair on her body stood on end. The chemistry that had been simmering between them since he had appeared on the beach was at combustion point, and her head spun with a dizzying mixture of trepidation and breathless excitement.

'What are you doing?' she mumbled when he

removed her glasses and put them back in his jacket pocket.

'Following my own mad impulse,' he growled, ignoring her shocked gasp when he suddenly jerked her up against his chest. 'The same impulse we both felt in the banqueting hall. Don't deny it, Rina,' he warned silkily when she frantically shook her head from side to side. 'I saw what was in your mind.'

Recalling her shamefully erotic fantasy, which had involved him sliding his hand beneath her skirt, and touching her where no man had ever touched her before, Kitty prayed he hadn't. But Nikos was lowering his head towards her, and it seemed to her shell-shocked brain as if everything were happening in slow motion. She tensed, torn between wanting to pull out of his arms and race back to the palace, and another, shocking need to stay and allow him to fulfil the determined intent in his dark gaze.

She moistened her suddenly dry lips with the tip of her tongue—and, watching her, Nikos felt his stomach muscles clench. This had been building since she had stood up to him earlier in the evening. He hadn't felt such a searing sexual attraction to a woman for a long time, and he dipped his head slowly, savouring the anticipation, and exploring the shape of her lips with his tongue before he claimed her mouth with a hunger he could no longer control.

Until the split second before Nikos slanted his mouth over hers, Kitty hadn't really believed he would kiss her, but her little gasp of shock was smothered beneath the pressure of his lips firmly coaxing hers apart. He was totally in control and he let her know it with the determined sweep of his tongue as he probed between her lips, demanding access to the moistness within. And she was powerless to stop him; lost from the moment he'd first touched her and caught up in a maelstrom of emotions as she felt the piercing sweetness of intense sexual desire for the first time in her life.

Nikos slid his hand round to Kitty's nape, tangled his fingers in her hair and tugged gently, angling her head so that he could deepen the kiss. Her response was instant and had a devastating affect on his libido so that he closed his other arm around her waist and dragged her hard up against the solid length of his arousal straining urgently beneath his trousers.

Rina was small and soft, and through his jacket he could feel the outline of her ripe curves that had proved such an unbearable temptation when she had stripped in the moonlight. She smelled of the sea; tasted of it too, he noted when he moved his mouth to her throat and stroked his tongue along her collarbone. He was used to women who wore designer clothes and drenched their skin in expensive perfumes, but there was something earthy, almost pagan, about this woman that struck a chord deep inside him. She was naturally sensual and totally in tune with her femininity, and instinct told him she would be a generous and adventurous lover.

His eyes were drawn to the deep valley of her cleavage and with a tortured groan he claimed her mouth once more, crushing her soft lips beneath his while he slid his hand into the front of his jacket and stroked his fingers lightly over one of her full, firm breasts.

He must have startled her because her whole body jerked with reaction, and, sensing her hesitation, he withdrew his hand, feeling a sharp tug of regret that he was denied the pleasure of caressing the erect point of her nipple. *Theos,* she was a sorceress; a sea-witch enticing him to forget everything but his desperation to sink his swollen shaft deep within her and possess her, but he could feel the sudden tension that gripped her, and calling on all his will power, he tore his mouth from hers and stared down at her, fighting for breath. 'This is madness,' he grated harshly. 'If either of us had any sense we should return to the palace. But my sanity seems to have deserted me, Rina, so the choice is yours. Will you end this now and go back? Or stay and drink champagne with me in the moonlight?'

It felt like a defining moment in her life, but Nikos had only asked her to drink champagne with him,

Kitty reassured herself as she snatched oxygen into her lungs and tried to control the frantic thudding of her heart. He was watching her intently, waiting for her answer, and she gave a little shiver. No man had ever asked her to drink champagne on a beach in the moonlight; no man had ever kissed her the way Nikos had, or stirred the passion that had been locked deep inside her for so long.

After a life spent adhering to duty and protocol Nikos Angelaki was like a breath of fresh air. He was dark and sexy and dangerous to know, but he made her feel daring—and the heat in his eyes made her feel desirable for the first time in her life.

She swallowed and forced herself to meet his gaze, feeling as though she were about to cast herself over the edge of a precipice. 'I love champagne,' she whispered shyly, shocked by her temerity.

He made no reply, and for a few agonising seconds she thought he had changed his mind and was going to send her away. But then he relaxed, and his slow smile stole her breath.

'Come, then,' he said, holding out his hand. His fingers closed around hers and even that tiny gesture was wonderfully new. She was twenty-six and she had never walked along a beach hand in hand with a lover, she thought despairingly. She didn't know where the years had gone, but it seemed as though one minute she had been a child and suddenly she was a grown woman who had been so absorbed with her studies and her work for the museum that romance and boyfriends had bypassed her.

She had taken on her share of royal commitments uncomplainingly because that was how she had been brought up: dutiful, obedient, always conscious of her position and grateful for the privileges that came with being a member of the royal family. But Nikos did not know she was a princess; he thought she was a waitress called Rina, and for a few hours she could be normal— just a woman who had met a man and was free to respond to the chemistry that smouldered between them.

The cave was illuminated by a lamp that he must have brought from the garden. The pale beam of light that spilled from it highlighted the sculpted beauty of his face, and Kitty felt a fluttering sensation in her chest as her eyes focused on the sensual curve of his mouth. She hovered uncertainly while he dropped down onto the dry sand, the common sense for which she was famed telling her to go—now—before she did something she would later regret. But her feet seemed to be melded to the floor of the cave, and when he patted the sand next to him she walked slowly forwards.

He held out a bottle of champagne. 'Here, have some. You're shivering again. It's a pity it isn't brandy, but I'm afraid you'll have to make do with vintage Bollinger.' He stretched out so that his lean, hard body was spread temptingly before her. His white silk shirt was open at the throat revealing the tanned column of his throat and a mass of dark body hair that she'd noticed also covered his forearms. He was so *male,* so overwhelmingly virile, Kitty thought shakily as she sank onto her knees beside him and took the bottle.

'It doesn't seem right to drink champagne from the bottle,' she murmured. 'It's very…decadent.'

'Decadent?' Nikos's low rumble of laughter echoed around the cave. 'What a curious mix of contradictions you are, Rina. You sound as prim as a Victorian governess, and yet you're happy to go skinny-dipping in the moonlight. Do I need to remind you that you are naked beneath my jacket?'

He couldn't remember the last time he had seen a woman blush, Nikos mused idly. The sexually confident women he dated were sophisticated game-players long past the first flush of virginal innocence. The thought caused him to frown as he watched Kitty take a sip of champagne. She seemed to be a curious mixture: shy one minute and eagerly responsive to him the next. When he had first kissed her he'd gained the impression that it was a new experience for her, but after her initial hesitation she had parted her mouth beneath his and kissed him back with such fiery passion that he had dismissed the idea.

He didn't need to remind himself that she was wearing nothing, he acknowledged grimly when she handed him the champagne bottle and he took a long draught. The dinner jacket was far too big for her and fastened so low that he could see the rounded contours of her breasts. He did not know what crazy impulse had made him ask her to stay, and he was already regretting it. He never made rash decisions. Even when he gambled he carefully weighed up the odds before he threw the dice. But for some reason Rina disturbed his cool, logical brain—and disturbed other areas of his body too. He wanted to kiss her again and never stop, but instead he forced himself to relax and tried to ignore the temptation of tasting champagne from her lips.

'So, Rina,' he queried lightly, 'what made you decide to become a waitress?'

Oh, Lord—how did she answer that? 'I…um, I need to work,' Kitty mumbled awkwardly, thinking that now might be a good time to bid him goodnight. 'Like most people, I have to earn a living, and I'm not trained to do anything else.' She thought of the years she'd spent studying for her degree, and her absorbing work at Aristo's museum, and tried to imagine what life would be like if she hadn't had the benefit of an excellent education, and really did have to work in some menial job. She had little idea of life outside her gilded cage, and although she supported various charities she couldn't imagine what it must be like to be poor. The only experience she'd had of life in the real world was when she had worked as a volunteer at Aristo's hospital, but, although she had found the work rewarding, her father had disapproved—citing concerns for her safety—and forbidden her from going.

'Have you always lived on Aristo?'

That was easier to answer, and Kitty nodded. 'I was born here, and I never want to live anywhere else. Aristo is the most beautiful place on earth.'

Nikos laughed. 'Have you visited many other places, then—on a waitress's pay?'

'Well…no,' Kitty faltered. She could hardly tell him that she had spent a year travelling around Europe and had visited Paris, Rome, cosmopolitan London, Venice and Florence, followed by six months at an exclusive finishing school in Switzerland. She had been a guest at royal palaces and country mansions, had wandered around fabulous art galleries and been taken on tours of all the famous sights, but nowhere compared to Aristo, the jewel of the Mediterranean. 'Aristo is my home and I love it here,' she told Nikos firmly.

Her passion for the island intrigued him, and he wondered why she felt so strongly about it. Was it the place or people that held her heart? 'Do you have a family here?' he asked curiously.

What would he say if she revealed that her family had ruled Aristo for generations? Kitty felt as though she were falling deeper and deeper into a mire. She wasn't lying exactly, she told herself. She just wasn't telling the whole truth. 'I have a mother, sister, brothers…' She faltered, thinking of the person who was missing from the list, and her heart contracted. 'My father died a few months ago.'

'I'm sorry.'

It wasn't a throwaway remark—Kitty heard the note of compassion in Nikos's voice, and tears, sudden and unbidden, stung her eyes. 'I miss him so much,' she admitted thickly. 'Sometimes I see his face in my mind, hear his voice, and I can't believe he isn't here any more.' She brushed her hand across her wet eyes, and was startled when Nikos captured her fingers in one of his strong hands and traced his thumb pad down her cheek, following the damp trail.

'I'm sorry.' She didn't want to cry in front of him. Her grief was a private matter that she shared with no one, not even her family. She had been especially close to the king, and he had called her his gentle dove, but she had been taught never to display her emotions. One of the golden rules of the royal family was to exert self-control at all times. Embarrassed by her weakness, she tried to draw away from Nikos but he curled his arm around her shoulders and tugged her towards him.

'Don't be sorry,' he said quietly. 'I know how devastating it is to lose a parent. My mother died many years ago, but I will never forget her. You won't forget your father, Rina, but the memories will become easier, and eventually you will think of him without the sadness you feel now.'

He smoothed her hair back from her face, and Kitty closed her eyes, soothed by the rhythmic stroking of his fingers. She felt his warm breath on her face and when she lifted her lashes she drowned in the depths of his midnight-dark gaze. He was so strong, so *alive,* and she wanted to absorb some of his strength because she felt weak and lost and achingly lonely inside.

Tentatively she rested her hand on his chest and felt the steady thud of his heart beneath her fingertips. It was utterly silent in the cave, as if they were cut off from the outside world and were the only two people in the universe. She could hear the sound of Nikos breathing—no longer steady but quicker, like his heartbeat; and she lifted her eyes to his face and stared at him, mesmerised by his masculine beauty.

Nikos knew he should move and break the spell

that had been cast on him in the witching hour, but his muscles were locked. In the lamplight the tears that spiked Rina's lashes glittered like tiny diamonds and the shadow of pain in her eyes moved him. It was more than fifteen years since his mother had died. He had been sixteen, a boy suddenly forced to be a man, but he still remembered the pain in his gut, the feeling that his insides had been ripped out, and the dull acceptance that the only person who had ever loved him had gone.

Rina's loss was clearly still raw, the unspoken plea in her eyes asked for comfort, and that was all Nikos intended to give when he lowered his head and brushed his mouth softly over hers. For a moment she did not respond, but neither did she pull away and he tasted her again, delicately, offering her the warmth of his body and silently letting her know that he understood the agony of grief. Even when she parted her mouth beneath his and tilted her head back a fraction for him to deepen the kiss he was sure he was in control. But her lips were so beguilingly soft and the temptation to dip his tongue between them and drink the lingering nectar of champagne became overwhelming.

Slowly he tightened his arm around her and slid his hand into her hair. It felt like silk against his skin and his heart began to pound with a thudding drumbeat of desire as he tangled his fingers in the chestnut strands and drew her closer still so that her breasts pushed against the wall of his chest.

Kitty couldn't pinpoint the exact moment when Nikos's kiss changed from a gentle caress that soothed her fragile emotions to one of hungry passion that stirred her soul and sent molten heat flooding through her veins. All she knew was that the pressure of his mouth increased and slid over hers with increasing urgency, and his tongue no longer traced the shape of her lips but thrust between them with a fierce demand that made her tremble.

The voice in her head warned her that she was heading into dangerous waters and she should pull back now, before she was swept away. But she did not want to move out of his arms and feel cold and alone again. She wanted him to hold her even closer so that she could absorb the warmth of his body, and she curled her hands around his neck and pressed herself against him, making no protest when he drew her down so that they were stretched out on the sand.

Now they were lying hip to hip, and the unmistakable evidence of Nikos's arousal jutting against her thighs caused her muscles to tense. This was wrong, very wrong, and it had to stop—now. But when he found her mouth once more in a slow, drugging kiss, she could not help but respond. Just a few more minutes in his arms, and then she would draw away from him, she promised herself. Surely it wasn't too much to ask—a few passionate kisses with the sexiest man she had ever met before she returned to her lonely life. But now she no longer felt relaxed, she was aware of a restless ache deep in her pelvis, and when he lifted his mouth from hers she gave a little murmur of protest.

'*Theos,* Rina!' Nikos's ragged voice echoed harshly in the cloistered quiet of the cave. 'This is insanity. You should leave while I still have some measure of control.' He stared down at her, his blood thundering in his veins when he saw the dazed passion in her eyes, and said slowly, 'Because if you do not, I can't guarantee that I will be able to stop.'

CHAPTER FOUR

NIKOS'S words were an unwelcome intrusion, slicing through the fog that clouded Kitty's brain. She didn't want to think, she wanted to feel and touch and lose herself in the world of sensory pleasure that his kisses evoked. She felt as though she were standing on the threshold of some new and wonderful place and Nikos was giving her the choice of stepping through the door, or closing it and turning back. Her mind flew to the royal ball and the loneliness she'd felt as she'd watched the couples on the dance floor. Everyone seemed to have a partner except her. All her friends were getting married and starting families but she had never even had a proper boyfriend. She recalled Vasilis Sarondakos's cruel taunts that she would end up a virgin spinster, and despair tugged her heart. She didn't want to be alone any more, and the flames of desire in Nikos's eyes told her that tonight she didn't have to be.

Tentatively she touched his face, and traced her finger across his mouth. She could hardly believe she was lying in the dark cave with the sexiest man she had ever met, and that sense of unreality numbed her to everything but her longing for him to kiss her again. Her innate shyness trapped her tongue, but the silent message in her eyes was enough for Nikos, and his chest heaved as he drew a harsh breath. The flare of feral hunger in his dark gaze sent a frisson of trepidation through Kitty, but then she forgot everything but the feel and touch and taste of him as he kissed her with an unrestrained hunger that warned her she had opened Pandora's box and had better be prepared for the consequences.

The feel of Nikos's hands brushing lightly against her skin as he unfastened the buttons on his jacket caused Kitty's heart to jerk frantically beneath her ribs, and doubt flooded through her. The memory of Vasilis roughly pawing her breasts filled her mind, and she tensed, her breath coming in sharp little gasps of panic. But Nikos was not rough, and the glitter of male appreciation in his eyes as he slowly pushed the edges of the jacket apart and revealed the pouting fullness of her breasts sent a shiver of another kind through Kitty. Her panic gradually receded as he gently cupped each breast in his palms and felt their weight and softness.

He muttered something indistinct beneath his

breath and colour flared briefly along his cheek-bones. 'Beautiful,' he said thickly, and stroked his fingertip across one nipple in a feather-light caress. The sensation was so exquisite that Kitty gasped and then closed her eyes and felt the pleasure build when he brushed his thumb pad lightly over the crest of her other breast.

Nikos guided her hands to the front of his shirt and aided her in freeing the buttons. Hands shaking, Kitty pushed the material aside to reveal his broad, muscular chest; olive-gold satin covered with whorls of dark hair that arrowed down over his taut abdomen. He drew her to him and she caught her breath at that very first contact of a hard male chest pressed against the softness of her breasts. It felt so good, so right, and so very seductive that she burrowed closer still, loving the strength of his arms around her as he found her mouth once more and kissed her until she was breathless.

Nikos had convinced himself that he was in control and that he would only allow things to go so far before he called a halt. He had occasionally had one-night stands: brief, mutually satisfying encounters with sexually confident women who, like him, wanted to answer a basic need without the complication of emotions. But those occasions had always been on his terms and, although the sex had invariably been enjoyable, he had never been driven by uncontrollable desire. For reasons he did not understand Rina was different. The raging need he felt to make love to her had never happened before and he was shocked to realise that he couldn't fight it.

Perhaps it was because she was so amazingly responsive and so unguarded in her pleasure when he caressed her? Frustrated by his inability to resist her, he gave her a hard, almost angry kiss, but she responded with such sweet passion that he gave up battling with himself and eased the pressure of his lips until the kiss evolved into a sensual tasting that became increasingly erotic. When she was utterly pliant in his arms he trailed his mouth lower, following the path of his hands to her breasts and drew lazy circles with his tongue around one nipple until it hardened to a taut peak.

The sensation of Nikos's mouth on her breast was indescribable, and when he drew her nipple fully into his mouth Kitty instinctively arched her back. She curled her fingers into his hair and gave a soft cry, shifting her hips restlessly beneath him as the tugging sensation on her breast became unbearably exquisite.

'Nikos…' His name left her lips as a whimpered plea and she tossed her head from side to side when he transferred his mouth to her other swollen crest and metered the same delicious torture.

He growled something she did not catch, but his intention became clear when he unfastened the last button of his jacket and spread the material to reveal the faint curve of her stomach and the triangle of dark curls clustered at the junction between her thighs. He moved so that he was kneeling above her, and Kitty blushed when he trailed his eyes deliberately down her body. The knowledge that he had watched her undress earlier was no help. She had been unaware of his presence, and even beneath the bright moon she must have been partly in shadow. Now she was completely exposed to him. No man had ever seen her body before, and desperate shyness, combined with her insecurities about her figure, caused her to try and shield herself with her hands.

It was time to end this craziness, Nikos acknowledged, trying to ignore the stomach-dipping sense of disappointment that clawed at his insides. He couldn't quite comprehend how they had got to this point. He'd had no intention of actually having sex with the waitress he'd met only hours before, but she was so sexy she would tempt a saint, let alone a mortal man who was burning up with sexual frustration.

But Rina had tensed, he could sense her uncertainty, and it would be unfair of him to try and persuade her to take their passion to its ultimate conclusion—even though he was certain that with patience and restraint he could arouse her to a level where she would willingly make love with him. Another moment and he would refasten the jacket and bring them both back down to reality, he told himself. He took a deep breath, nostrils flaring as he fought for control, but he could not resist stroking his hand lightly over her stomach, and then lower.

Her thighs were silky smooth, and he caught her faint gasp when he brushed his fingers through her silky curls. 'Why do you want to hide yourself from me?' he murmured huskily. 'You have a beautiful body, Rina. I'm sure you can be in no doubt that I'm massively turned on by you,' he added self-derisively, knowing that she could hardly miss the throbbing hardness of his erection pressed against her thigh.

'Are you?' her breathy little voice whispered in the silent cave and Nikos stiffened, thinking that she was taunting him. But there was no hint of teasing in the big brown eyes that were focused on him. She reminded him of a timid deer that was poised for flight, and yet, with gentle handling, might stay and allow him closer.

'What do you think?' he said quietly as he took her hand and laid it over the bulge beneath his trousers. He watched her eyes widen, her pupils hugely dilated, and could not resist lowering his head and kissing her softly swollen mouth. The feel of her lips parting beneath his threatened to shatter his self-control, and, tempted beyond bearing, he slid his hand between her legs and delicately probed the tightly closed edge of her femininity. Her whole body jerked with reaction, and he thought for a moment that she would reject him, but then she slowly relaxed, and his blood thundered in his veins when he gently parted her and discovered the unmistakable evidence of her arousal.

Kitty's heart was beating so fast that she was sure it would burst through her chest as she felt Nikos part her, and she caught her breath when he slowly inserted a finger between her silken folds. She could feel the betraying dampness between her legs and was embarrassed that he would know she was aroused, but he gave a low growl of satisfaction and eased deeper inside her while his thumb pad found the tight little nub of her clitoris and tenderly stroked across it with devastating effect.

'Oh…' The shock of experiencing her first intimate male caress caused Kitty to cry out. The feel of Nikos's finger moving inside her was bliss, rapture beyond anything she had ever imagined, and she trembled as intense sensations rippled through her. To her untutored body it seemed impossible that there could be more, that she wasn't already at the peak, but the ache deep inside her was growing ever more demanding, and following an instinct as old as time she tried clumsily to pull him down on top of her.

'Wait, *agape*.' His voice was hoarse, as if he too was no longer in control of himself and was driven by a deeply ingrained, basic need that could no longer be denied. Kitty did not know how he divested himself of his clothes without her being aware of it, but suddenly he was naked and he spread the edges of his jacket that she was still wearing wide open and came down on her, the rough hairs that covered his thighs and abdomen feeling slightly abrasive against her skin. She felt the jutting length of his penis press into her belly—so shockingly rigid and alien to her that her eyes flew open and she stared up at him as he loomed over her, and swallowed at the hard gleam in his eyes.

What on earth was she doing? Was she really going to allow Nikos—a man she had never met until tonight—to make love to her? A tremor ran through her. She shouldn't be here, should never have allowed the fiery attraction between them to burst into flame. Nikos was a notorious playboy and she was a princess from the royal house of Karedes—yet even knowing that it was wrong, she acknowledged with searing honesty that she didn't want Nikos to stop.

'*I bet you're still a virgin.*' Vasilis's sneering

voice echoed in her head, and rebellion flared in her heart. She was twenty-six, and it was time she became a woman, but out of fairness to Nikos she knew she must confess her inexperience.

'Nikos,' she whispered faintly, 'I think I should tell you…' But the rest of her words were lost beneath his mouth as he claimed her lips in a searing, soul-shattering kiss that dismantled the last of her doubts and fears.

'Tell me what?' he muttered. 'You're not on the Pill—is that it? Don't worry. I'll take care of it.' The sensual smokiness of his voice wrapped around Kitty like a cocoon, and she was only dimly conscious of him reaching into his jacket pocket and donning protection with a swift efficiency that spoke of plenty of practice. Then he came down on her once more, settled his hard, muscular body between her thighs, and she could feel the pulsing thickness of his shaft press impatiently against her opening.

This was it, the moment she had wondered about all of her adult life, and she still couldn't quite believe that it was going to happen. Her heart was galloping, her breath coming in short, shallow pants, and suddenly her nerve deserted her and she tried to bring her legs together. But she was too late, Nikos was already surging forwards, and he gently but firmly pushed her thighs apart and entered her with one deep, powerful thrust that brought a shocked cry from Kitty's lips.

'*Theos!*' He stilled instantly and stared down at her, his brows lowering in a harsh frown. 'Your first time? How can it be?' Nikos demanded in stunned incomprehension. He began to withdraw from her, but now that Kitty was over the first shock of penetration her muscles were stretching around him and the brief pain was fading. She loved the new and wondrous sensation of having him fill her completely, and the restless ache inside her was once again clamouring to be assuaged.

'Don't stop…please.' She clung to his shoulders, urging him down again, and, sensing his indecision, she wrapped her legs around him, inviting him to push into her once more. It was an invitation he couldn't refuse and with a muttered imprecation he surged forward, taking it slower this time, but the power of each ensuing thrust was no less intense and Kitty arched beneath him and gave herself up to the pleasure of feeling him move within her.

Deeper, harder, Nikos was aware that he was losing control, and he slipped his hands under her and cupped her bottom, lifting her so that he could plunge deeper still, setting a rhythm that was fast and frantic as he took them both to the edge.

The burning ache in her pelvis was unbearable

now, and Kitty felt as if something inside her were being stretched until it could be stretched no more and it would snap at any second. 'Please…' She couldn't stand it any longer. It had to happen, *now*. She curled her fingers into the sweat-dampened hair at Nikos's nape and clung to him while he drove into her again and again, taking her higher and increasing her excitement with every stroke.

And suddenly, when she was trembling and desperate, he gave one more devastating thrust, and the dam burst. A tidal wave of pleasure swept through her as her muscles contracted in pulse after pulse of exquisite sensation, and the ripples radiated out until every inch of her body was suffused in ecstasy. Almost simultaneously she heard the low groan that seemed to be ripped from his throat and felt the great shudders that tore through him as he reached his own release. He slumped on top of her and she felt his heart slamming in his chest.

In a protective gesture as old as womankind she crossed her arms over his back and cradled him on her breasts, holding him tight for those few moments while he was at his most vulnerable. Tears filled her eyes and tenderness swamped her heart. He had just given her the most incredible experience of her life and in the aftermath she felt as though their souls as well as their bodies had been as one. It seemed impossible that he did not feel it too. But too soon he raised himself onto his elbows and stared down at her, the gleam in his eyes no longer caused by passion, but anger, as he demanded, 'Why the *hell* didn't you tell me you were a virgin?'

Kitty took one look at Nikos's grim expression and swiftly dismissed the idea that the intense passion they had just shared had meant anything more to him than a physical release of lust. This feeling that their souls had meshed and were now inextricably entwined was an illusion brought on by the intensity of her first sexual experience, and the coldness in his eyes warned her he did not share her fantasy.

Now that the heat of passion was cooling she felt faintly sick, and her limbs were trembling uncontrollably with shocked reaction to what had happened, but pride dictated that she hide her emotional turmoil from Nikos.

'It was my business,' she murmured lightly, striving to sound as though giving him her virginity was no big deal.

Nikos was not appeased. 'But now you have made it my business,' he said harshly. 'I am not in the habit of seducing virgins. If you had told me, I would have stopped.'

'But I didn't want you to stop,' Kitty admitted

quietly, silently acknowledging the truth of her statement. The strength of passion he had aroused in her had been a revelation, and for those few wild moments she had forgotten everything but her need for fulfilment. It was only now that the self-recriminations were queuing up in her head.

Nikos had rolled off her and was now watching her intently, his eyes narrowed and suspicious on her face. Intuitively she knew what was bothering him. He was a playboy with a well-publicised aversion to commitment. She guessed he was wondering what she might want from him, and was doubtless determined to impress on her that he would give her nothing. Perhaps he feared that she would turn clingy and emotional? He wasn't to know that she would rather die than allow him to see how much he affected her.

Feeling acutely self-conscious now, she tugged the edges of his jacket together, flushing beneath his sardonic look that said it was a little too late for modesty. 'If you want the honest truth, my virginity had become something of a hindrance,' she told him, hoping she sounded confident and convincing, rather than perilously close to tears. 'I wanted my first time to be an enjoyable experience, but I wanted a man, not some clumsy, inexperienced boy. Your reputation as an expert lover was a temptation I couldn't resist, and I certainly wasn't disappointed—' her voice faltered slightly

'—but I apologise if my performance and experience were less than you'd expected.'

'Don't be ridiculous. I wasn't disappointed, as I'm sure—despite your inexperience—you must have noticed,' he responded dryly, remembering the shattering intensity of his release. 'You were amazing, *agape.*'

Nikos shifted onto his back and stared up at the shadows flickering on the roof of the cave. The stark shock of discovering that he was her first lover was fading, and he acknowledged that it had been the best sex he'd had for a long time. He glanced at Rina lying beside him and slowly relaxed, relieved that she had made no attempt to cuddle up to him. It seemed that he had no need to worry. She had been a virgin but she understood the rules. He hadn't intended to see her again after tonight, but if she could be trusted not to make demands on him then he saw no reason why they shouldn't meet up occasionally when he came to Aristo.

'I also have a confession to make,' he said lazily as he rolled onto his side once more and wound a lock of her still-damp hair around his finger.

Kitty's heart shuddered to a standstill. 'Are you married?'

He gave a snort of disgust. '*Theos*—no!' Nikos's face hardened, and he suddenly seemed so remote that Kitty wondered despairingly what utter madness had led her to have sex for the first time in her life with this man who was a stranger to her. 'I'm divorced,' he told her with a grim smile that did not reach his eyes, 'and, since I evicted my ex-wife from my life, resolutely single.'

Nikos felt the familiar black hatred surge through him as his mind dwelled on the woman he had once believed he had loved, his bitterness mixed with fury with himself that he had been such a damnable fool. Never again, he thought savagely. Greta's terrible deceit had taught him a hard lesson, but he had learned it well. Never trust any woman or invest emotion in them, because, as he had found out in the cruellest way imaginable, they weren't worth it.

He jerked his thoughts from the past and realised that Rina was staring at him. His eyes narrowed on her startled expression. 'If you're harbouring any romantic illusions about me, then I suggest you forget them fast, *agape*. I value my freedom above everything.'

Kitty was silent for a moment, trying to assimilate the knowledge that he had been married. It was the first real thing she had learned about him, and she couldn't help feeling shocked and—even more ridiculous—crushingly disappointed. She couldn't picture him married—it didn't fit with his image. She wondered what his wife had been like. Stunningly beautiful, of course, she brooded. Probably a glamorous model like the women he was frequently photographed in the papers with.

She was curious about the reasons why the marriage had ended. Nikos had been unable to hide the bitter note in his voice when he had spoken of his ex-wife. Whatever had happened in his past had clearly had a huge impact on him and his relationships since his divorce, because his affairs were numerous and short-lived, and a few of his ex-lovers who had sold their story to the tabloids had stated that he had a heart of granite.

She glanced up to find him watching her, the expression in his dark eyes unfathomable. Inside she felt in turmoil, but she managed a careless shrug. 'Lucky I stopped believing in fairy tales long ago, then. I have no illusions about the kind of man you are, Nikos. But I'm still curious to hear your confession.'

The brief tension between them passed, she saw Nikos visibly relax and his seductive smile sent a quiver of reaction through her. 'I didn't have permission from the Prince Regent to come down to the beach, either,' he drawled.

'Then how did you know about the path from the palace?' Kitty asked, confused.

'My mother told me about it when I was a child. I was walking in the gardens tonight when I suddenly remembered her saying that there was a secret path to the beach, and I decided to look for it, not knowing for sure if the story was true, or simply a rumour she had heard when she—' He broke off abruptly, and then, in answer to Kitty's bewildered stare, added, 'When she lived here on Aristo.'

There was no particular reason why he should not tell Rina that his mother had been a servant at the palace, Nikos conceded. If anything, it was rather ironic that he had been drawn to a member of the palace staff rather than one of the sophisticated guests at the ball. Perhaps he had a secret desire to return to his roots, he thought dryly. But his personal life was his own, and for all he knew Rina might decide to sell her story of how she had met him to the tabloids. MY SEX SESSION ON THE SAND WITH GREEK TYCOON might be a headline grabber, but a revelation that Nikos Angelaki was the illegitimate child of a palace servant would sell even better, and he refused to have his mother's reputation smeared in some sleazy rag.

'I thought you are Greek?' Kitty murmured, eager to learn more about him.

'My mother was born and grew up on Aristo. She came from around the bay, at a place called Varna.'

Kitty knew every part of Aristo, and she frowned as she thought of the tiny fishing village where Nikos had said his mother had lived. There were a few big estates on the hills above Varna, and she supposed his family owned one of them. 'I know you said your mother died some years ago, but do you visit her family often?'

'No.' Nikos's jaw hardened as he thought of the relatives he had never met—his mother's family who had thrown her out when she had fallen pregnant with him. None of them were left now. According to the private detective he had employed to trace them, his grandmother had died years ago, and his grandfather had passed away at the ripe age of eighty-six—without ever knowing that he had a grandson, and taking the identity of Nikos's father with him to the grave.

Nikos's mother had steadfastly refused to tell him the name of the man who had made her pregnant and then abandoned her—revealing only that he had been a Greek fisherman. It wasn't a lot to go on, Nikos acknowledged grimly. Realistically he accepted that there was no chance he would ever know who had sired him, but that didn't stop him wondering whose blood ran through his veins.

'My mother's family are all dead,' he told Kitty, his tone warning her that he did not want to continue the discussion. He rolled onto his back once more, suddenly feeling dog-tired. God knew how many hours it had been since he had boarded a plane at Dubai International Airport, but jet lag was catching up with him and his eyelids felt heavy. He wouldn't go to sleep, he promised himself. He would just rest his eyes for a couple of minutes…

Kitty listened to the rhythmic sound of Nikos breathing and carefully inched away from him. He looked curiously vulnerable in sleep and she longed to brush the lock of black hair back from his brow. He was so gorgeous; she could sit and look at him for ever, but what would happen when he woke up? Her face burned as she imagined them casually pulling on their clothes and strolling back to the palace. She supposed he would bid her goodnight—maybe even kiss her again? She had been trained in the rules of etiquette but she had no knowledge of the rules of lovers.

Would Nikos ask to see her again or ask for her phone number? *At what point would she tell him that she was Princess Katarina, his best friend's sister—and not a waitress called Rina?*

She should never have lied to him, she thought desperately. But when she had met him at the ball and allowed him to think she was a servant she'd had no idea that they would be lovers before the night was out. The enormity of what she had done struck her with the force of a tidal wave and she held her hand against her mouth to hold back her cry of despair. She had to go now, before Nikos woke up.

Heart racing, she scrambled to her feet and

groped for her glasses. Nikos had placed her clothes on a rock and she quickly slipped off his jacket and folded it neatly next to him before she dragged her dress over her head, not daring to waste precious time fumbling with her under-wear.

She realised that her shoes must still be down by the shore, but Nikos could stir at any minute, and so she ran barefoot to the back of the cave, out through the narrow hole in the rocks and up the path leading back to the palace. Heart pounding, she fled through the dark, thankful that she knew every twist and turn and half expecting to hear Nikos coming after her. But there was no sound of his footfall and she flew across the garden and into the palace through the now empty kitchens.

The party was over and the guests had gone. The caterers had left, and the palace staff had all retired for the night. No one saw her on her way up to her bedroom but her heart felt as though it would burst when she locked her door and stag-gered over to the mirror to stare at the reflection of the woman she barely recognised as herself, with her swollen mouth and her hair tumbling in wild disarray over her shoulders.

What had she done? She must have been out of her mind. Nikos had invited her to drink cham-pagne with him but she'd barely had a sip and couldn't blame alcohol for her appalling behaviour. Kitty buried her face in her hands, as if she could somehow blot out the memories of the wild passion she had shared with Nikos in the cave. God knew what he must think of her. But it couldn't be any worse than her opinion of herself. She was just thankful she was never likely to see him again. She could never risk him discovering her true identity. It was far better that he believed he'd had a one-night stand with a lowly domestic assistant called Rina—and for her to forget she had ever met him.

CHAPTER FIVE

IN THE days following the royal ball Kitty did her best to banish Nikos from her mind—but failed hopelessly. Every time she closed her eyes she saw his face, and at night she dreamed she was in his arms, their bodies intimately entwined.

Sexual frustration was a new and unwelcome experience, but soon another reason kept her awake until the early hours. Her period was late— and she had always been as regular as clockwork. As the days passed with no sign that would put her mind at rest she acknowledged that it was no good trying to ignore her fears. But buying a pregnancy-test kit was no simple task for a member of the ruling family of Aristo. She was one of the lesser-known royals, but she couldn't just waltz into a chemist and brazenly buy a kit.

Eventually she drove into the centre of Ellos, Aristo's thriving capital city, and, hiding behind large sunglasses and an oversized sunhat, bought a kit from a busy outlet before swiftly leaving the shop, terrified that someone had recognised her. The test result was horribly predictable, and at the same time utterly shocking, and two weeks after the royal ball she stood in her bathroom and stared numbly at the blue line that had appeared on the pregnancy kit, wondering if the churning sensation in her stomach was caused by fear, or whether it was the first physical indication that she was expecting Nikos's baby. How could it be possible? she thought despairingly. Nikos had used protection. She felt as though she were caught in a nightmare from which there was no escape, and she wanted to bury her head under the duvet and wait for morning to come. But this wasn't a bad dream, this was real, and she had to face the fact that she was an unmarried, pregnant princess.

She was still in a state of shocked disbelief when Sebastian found her in the library later that morning. 'Ah, there you are, Kitty.' He stared at her closely. 'Are you okay? You've been looking pale for the past few days and Mama is concerned about you.'

'I'm fine,' Kitty said quickly. She swung away from Sebastian's sharp glance but not before he'd glimpsed the sheen of tears in her eyes.

'Hey, Kitty-Kat, what's the matter?'

'Nothing.' Her brother's gentle concern and his

use of her childhood nickname tore at Kitty's frayed emotions, and she dropped her head in her hands, great sobs racking her as the dam holding back her fears burst.

'*Kitty!* What the hell is it?' Sebastian's voice was harsh with anxiety as he walked round the desk and put his arm around her shoulders. 'Come on, you can tell me. Whatever it is it can't be *that* bad,' he coaxed softly. 'And you know I'll always help you.'

Sebastian had always been her protector, but even he couldn't sort out this problem. There was no way of lessening the impact of her announcement so she said starkly, 'I'm pregnant.'

For a few seconds the silent library seemed to echo with Sebastian's shock before he exploded into speech. '*What*? What do you mean?' he demanded, staring at her as if she had suddenly grown another head. 'I don't understand.'

For some reason his stunned incomprehension caused the truth to finally sink into Kitty's brain and she took a deep, shuddering breath. 'It's quite simple. I'm going to have a baby.'

Once again Sebastian was rendered speechless, but finally he straightened up, his jaw rigid as he asked with deadly softness, 'Whose baby?'

Nikos's arrogantly handsome face filtered into Kitty's mind. 'I can't tell you that,' she whispered miserably.

'Don't be ridiculous—' Sebastian broke off and

frowned. 'Are you saying you *don't* know? That the father could be one of several partners? *Theos*, Kitty, do you have a whole secret life that I know nothing about?'

'*No*...of course not,' she cried, more tears falling at the flare of disappointment in Sebastian's eyes. 'I know who the baby's father is—it could only be one person,' she said thickly. 'But it was an accident, a mistake and he...he won't be pleased. I've decided not to tell him.'

'I don't give a damn if he's pleased or not,' Sebastian growled, swinging away from her and raking his hand through his hair. 'It's you I'm concerned about. Kitty...' He broke off and closed his eyes briefly at the sight of her tear-streaked face. 'You are a royal princess of the House of Karedes. You are fourth in line to the throne, and you cannot be a single mother.'

Kitty bit her lip. It was no wonder Sebastian looked devastated. On the night of the ball Vasilis Sarondakos had taunted her that the royal family could not afford to be tainted by another scandal. No member of the ruling family of Aristo had ever given birth to an illegitimate child, and the implications could rock the House of Karedes to its foundations.

But her choices were limited; in fact they were non-existent. She was pregnant, and *not* having her baby was absolutely not a consideration.

Involving Nikos was another matter. He was Sebastian's closest friend, she thought despairingly, her heart cracking at her brother's shattered expression. How much worse would Sebastian feel if she revealed that she had been seduced by a man he trusted implicitly?

And she had lied to Nikos. She had allowed him to believe she was a waitress called Rina. How would he react if she revealed that, not only was she a royal princess, but that during their brief, sexual pairing she had conceived his child?

If you're harbouring any romantic illusions about me, then I suggest you forget them fast, he'd warned her immediately after he'd made love to her. *I value my freedom above everything.*

This was her problem and she would have to deal with it alone. She would have to retire from public duties and live quietly somewhere away from the palace. Financially she had the security of an annuity from her father, and when her child was older her qualifications would hopefully enable her to resume her career as a researcher at the museum. She took a deep breath and felt a sense of calm replace her earlier panic. Everything would be okay; she would cope. But she had no intention of ever revealing the identity of her baby's father—even to her family.

'Sebastian, I'm sorry but I can't tell you.' Kitty jumped to her feet and the colour drained from her face as a wave of dizziness swept over her. 'You'll have to excuse me. I'm not feeling very well,' she muttered as she hurried towards the door.

'What about Mama?' Sebastian's voice stopped her. 'She'll have to be told about this—and coming so soon after Papa's death it will break her heart. *Theos*, Kitty, what a mess,' he muttered grimly.

His stark words filled Kitty with guilt and shame. 'I will speak to Mama and the rest of the family. Just give me a few days to…to come to terms with things myself. Please, Seb.'

Sebastian hesitated, his gaze locked with her tear-filled eyes, and then he nodded abruptly. 'But if I ever find out who the father is, I swear I'll tear him limb from limb,' he vowed savagely. 'You deserve better than this, Kitty.'

A week later Kitty stood on the palace balcony, waving to the crowds who had gathered for the Day of Independence celebration that marked the day the Adamas Islands had gained independence from British rule. Queen Tia, still consumed with grief for her husband, had a chest infection and had been advised by her doctors not to attend. Prince Alex and his wife Maria were in America, and Prince Andreas was with his new wife Holly in her native Australia. Liss had other royal duties elsewhere to deal with and so Kitty had assured Sebastian that she would act as his consort—

aware that once she was a single mother she would no longer appear at state occasions.

Saturday was a beautiful June day typical of early summer in Aristo. Warm sunshine bathed the crowds who had followed the carnival procession through the streets, and as they flocked into the palace courtyard Kitty smiled and tried to ignore the discomfort of her heavy silk state gown and the ornate diamond tiara on her brow that had given her a headache.

'I don't think I've ever seen such a huge crowd of well-wishers. Hundreds of people have come to show their support for you, Sebastian,' she commented as she stepped off the balcony, into the drawing room, peeling off her white gloves as she walked and handing them to a footman. Her brother was chatting with a guest but at the sound of her voice he swung round—and as Kitty caught sight of his companion her heart stopped beating. If was as if someone had pressed the mute button. The voices of the people around her faded, and she was conscious of the fractured sound of her breathing and a peculiar rushing sound in her ears.

'Nikos, I don't think you actually met my sister at the ball a few weeks ago. This is Princess Katarina…' Sebastian fell silent, plainly bemused by Nikos Angelaki's coldly furious expression and Kitty's sudden pallor. The tense silence between them caused a ripple to run through the room, and Kitty felt the curious stares of the assembled guests, but her wide, shocked eyes were locked on Nikos's face.

He was the first to speak. 'Oh, we met, my friend,' he drawled in an icy tone that sent a shiver down Kitty's spine. His eyes narrowed, and Kitty could feel the aggression that emanated from him. 'But it seems that Princess Katarina likes to play games, and regrettably she neglected to properly introduce herself—didn't you, *Rina?*'

Shock surged like a foaming torrent through Nikos's blood, and with it a black rage that threatened to choke him. The woman who had come in from the balcony and was staring at him fearfully was instantly recognisable when she had spent the past three weeks lodged in his brain—and yet, dressed in her royal robes and tiara, she was someone he did not know.

She had lied to him that night on the beach. How she had lied! He closed his eyes briefly and tried to get a grip on the savage anger that made him want to shake her and demand an explanation as to *why* she had pretended to be a servant, instead of telling him at the start that she was Princess Katarina Karedes.

Had she found the pretence amusing? Fury burned corrosively in his gut. And why the *hell* had she slept with him? Not slept, he corrected himself grimly. She hadn't slept in his arms, she'd had sex with him—and even then she had lied by omission when she had failed to warn him she was a virgin. But he had slept. Overcome with exhaustion, and physically sated after making love to her, he had felt more relaxed than he had done in years and had been unable to fight the tiredness that had settled on him. When he had stirred again he'd discovered that an hour had passed, and Rina had disappeared.

Memories of the wild passion they had shared filled his mind. And another memory, of the private conversation he'd had with Sebastian when he had first arrived at the palace today, caused his heart to crash in his chest. Sebastian had been tense and grim-faced, and at first Nikos had assumed his friend was uptight about the fact that he had still not located the Stefani diamond. But the prince had wanted to confide in him about another matter, and had sworn him to secrecy before revealing that another scandal was about to rock the House of Karedes. His sister, Princess Katarina, had been seduced by some unknown man, and was pregnant.

Theos, no! It could not be true. He stared at Rina—unable to think of her as Princess Katarina—and tried to decipher the truth from her pale face. Not again, not to him. Not after the tragedy of his past that he would never forget for as long as he lived. But he knew instantly that this was no cruel trick. It was entirely possible that Rina had conceived his baby, and from the frown forming on Sebastian's brow it was clear that his friendship with the prince was about to be blown to pieces.

Kitty could not tear her eyes from Nikos's face, and the glittering fury in his dark gaze filled her with trepidation. He could not possibly guess her secret, she assured herself. But her hand moved instinctively to her stomach and she saw his eyes narrow as he witnessed the betraying gesture.

Sebastian was speaking, but his words did not register in Kitty's brain as she watched his concerned expression change to one of dawning comprehension followed by stunned fury. The rushing sound in her ears grew louder, as if she were standing at the edge of a waterfall. And then she was falling, and a great dark nothingness rushed up to meet her.

Kitty slowly opened her eyes and stared up at the fresco of cherubs that adorned the ceiling. For a moment she felt disorientated, but then her brain clicked into gear—and her memory returned with a vengeance. She turned her head to look around and realised that she was in the small ante-room leading from the formal drawing room. She recalled the blanket of black nothingness that had enveloped her, and understood. She must have fainted, for the first time in her life, and someone had carried her in here and placed her on the sofa. That someone was now silhouetted against the bright sunlight streaming in through the window, and even though she could not discern his features she was conscious of the waves of anger emanating from him.

Nikos! She swung her legs off the sofa and jerked upright, and then gasped as a wave of nausea swept over her. To be sick in front of him would be the ultimate humiliation, and she gritted her teeth and waited while the room righted itself and her head stopped spinning.

'There is a glass of water on the table next to you. I suggest you drink some,' he said in a terse voice. Kitty reached for the glass and lifted it to her lips. Her hands were shaking so much that she could barely take a sip, but the water was ice-cold and refreshing, and gradually the sickness passed. She stood up and risked a furtive glance across the room, and could not restrain a startled cry when she saw the livid bruise on Nikos's jaw.

'What happened to your face?'

'Sebastian,' he informed her shortly.

Kitty shook her head disbelievingly. 'He *hit* you?' She recalled the expression of shocked understanding she'd seen on her brother's face just before she had slipped into unconsciousness, and a heavy dread filled her.

'After the news he's just given me I don't blame him,' Nikos said, still in that cold, clipped voice that could not disguise his fury. 'In case you're worried, I did not retaliate. Sebastian was defending your honour, and to be honest I would have thought less of him if he hadn't taken a swing at me.' He paused, and in the tense silence the ticking clock and the sound of Kitty's heartbeat both sounded over-loud to her ears.

'But all things considered, it was a rather dramatic way to learn that I am going to be a father,' he drawled—sarcasm his only outlet for the murderous rage burning inside him, because if he lost control and vented his fury at the top of his voice he would alert the palace guards standing on duty outside the door. 'With you passing out, and the Prince Regent giving a good impression of a prize knuckle-fighter in front of a hundred or so dignitaries and members of the press, the story is likely to make the newspaper headlines worldwide.'

Nikos sucked in a harsh breath and swung round to stare blindly out of the window. Below, in the courtyard, the crowds were dispersing and streaming through the palace gates, many clutching flags bearing the national colours of Aristo and the coat of arms of the House of Karedes. He felt a deepening sense of unreality, a feeling that his life was about to change irrevocably, but he knew he must bring his anger under control and establish the real facts.

'Is it true?' His voice rasped in his throat, and he had to force himself to turn away from the window. 'Are you really pregnant, or are you playing another peculiar game of charades?'

'It's true,' Kitty choked, forcing the words past her numb lips. 'I did a test, and yesterday my doctor confirmed it.'

She did not know how she had expected Nikos to react. She hadn't dared picture a scenario in which she told him she had conceived his child, let alone imagined what he would say. He was clearly shocked, and she could understand that he might be angry, but the icy rage in his eyes shook her.

'And is the child mine, as Sebastian seems to think?'

His harsh tone triggered a flare of anger inside Kitty, and she flushed. 'Of course it's yours. I was a virgin when I met you and I haven't leapt into bed with half a dozen lovers since then. I didn't want to involve you. I don't even understand *how* I can be pregnant,' she added, dropping her eyes from his cold stare. 'You used protection.'

'It failed,' Nikos said bluntly. 'I discovered when I woke up that there was a slim chance I could have made you pregnant. When I realised you had left the cave I searched for you, fearing you may have gone for another swim and got into trouble in the current. It was only when I saw your clothes had gone that I faced the fact that you had run out on me.

'If you had stayed I would have told you there was a possibility you could have conceived, and insisted we kept in contact until we knew either way,' he finished curtly.

Nikos drew a ragged breath, recalling his concern in the days after he had had sex with Rina in the cave that a faulty contraceptive could have resulted in a child. When he had tried to trace her, and found that she seemed to have disappeared from the planet, his concern had turned to a gut-wrenching fear he could not dismiss, despite telling himself that history could not repeat itself.

Now he knew that it could.

Memories of the past that he had ruthlessly suppressed for so long surged into his mind. Five years ago his lover had fallen pregnant with his child. During his relationship with Greta he had confided that he felt as though a part of his identity was missing because he did not know who his father was, and he had vowed he would not abandon a woman if she fell pregnant with his child. Soon after, when Greta had revealed she was expecting his baby, he had immediately proposed. But his desire to marry the Danish model had not only been for the sake of the child.

He had loved her, Nikos acknowledged grimly. After his mother's death, work had become his obsession and he had never allowed any of his lovers to get too close. But Greta had been different. Their affair had been Nikos's longest relationship, and he had finally admitted that the beautiful blonde had got beneath his guard and captured his heart.

After his initial shock he had been glad about the baby, knowing that his child would be his only blood relation in the world. But a month after he and Greta had married, tragedy had occurred. To his dying day he would never forget her phone call from Denmark, where she had gone for a modelling assignment, telling him that she had miscarried.

Nikos stared blindly out of the palace window, remembering the sorrow that had swamped him. It had been a bitter blow, but he had dealt with his grief privately, and done his best to comfort Greta—unaware that her tears had been an act. In the months that had followed she had appeared to recover well, and quickly returned to modelling. But it had not been long before cracks appeared in their relationship. Greta loved to party, and had accused him of being a boring Greek husband. And she had been adamant that she wanted to concentrate on her career when Nikos had suggested they should try for another child.

Her open use of cocaine, and her revelation

that she had hidden her habit before their marriage, had led to a series of increasingly bitter rows, and it had been during one of her drug-fuelled rages that Greta had screamed the truth at him. She had never wanted a baby—but when she had fallen pregnant, and Nikos had proposed, she had seized her chance to marry a multi-millionaire. She had waited until after the wedding, but on her trip to Denmark she hadn't miscarried their child—she had chosen to terminate her pregnancy.

Nikos swallowed the bile in his throat, and forced his mind away from his ex-wife. Greta was in the past. The newspaper reports two years ago of her death from a drug overdose had elicited no sympathy from him. From the moment he'd learned how she had callously deprived him of his child his heart had frozen over, and, although he was a living, breathing man, inside he was emotionless and cold.

But he did not feel dead inside now. For the first time in five years something stirred within him, and he stared at the woman who had sworn she was carrying his baby, his heart pounding. Fate had given him another chance, another child—and he would move heaven and earth to ensure that the tiny speck of life created from his seed would have a chance of life.

CHAPTER SIX

KITTY stared numbly at Nikos, shaken by the bleakness in his eyes. He looked *devastated* by the news that she was expecting his baby. His jaw was rigid, his skin stretched so taut over his sharp cheekbones that he looked as though he had been carved from marble—cold and hard and utterly unforgiving.

The idea of fatherhood definitely did not appeal to him—that much was clear, she brooded bitterly. The tiny flame of hope that had lurked deep in her subconscious was snuffed out and pride made her voice strong. 'Don't look so worried, Nikos. I don't want anything from you. This is my problem, and I'll deal with it. You needn't be involved.'

Something flared in his eyes, an emotion Kitty could not define but that made her feel as though her legs were about to give way, and she sank weakly back down on the sofa.

'*Deal with it?*' he said in a dangerous tone.

'You are talking about a human life. In what way were you planning to deal with it?'

'I meant that I will take care of the baby, financially and in every other way,' Kitty faltered. 'What do you think I meant?' Her eyes widened as the implication of his words hit her, and sickness surged through her. 'You can't possibly think…' She took a shaky breath, but when she spoke her voice was fierce. 'I am having this baby, and as far as I'm concerned there is no viable alternative I would *ever* consider. But as I said before, you don't have to be involved.'

Nikos felt some of the terrible tension that had gripped him lessen. She had sounded convincing, but Rina, or Katarina as he now knew her, was an accomplished actress—he had evidence of that. 'But I am involved,' he said implacably, his eyes locked with hers. 'You are carrying my child, and I have a responsibility towards both of you that I fully intend to honour.'

He thought again of how she had deceived him, and was swamped by another wave of bitter anger. 'When were you going to tell me? Or weren't you going to bother? It would have been difficult, I suppose, when you had lied about your identity,' he added scathingly.

Kitty flushed and hung her head. 'I haven't known what to do these past few weeks,' she admitted huskily.

Nikos gave her a savage glance. 'While you were trying to decide, I was doing my best to find you. I made enquiries at the palace, but when I was told there was no employee here called Rina I contacted all the catering companies on Aristo. I'm sure you won't be surprised to hear that nobody had ever heard of you,' he drawled acidly. He paused, his dark brows lowered in a slashing frown. 'So tell me, *Rina*, do you often masquerade as a servant, or did you deliberately set out to make a fool of me?'

'I didn't…' Kitty bit her lip when she caught the glittering anger in his eyes. 'You have every right to be angry,' she admitted honestly.

'Well, that's good to know—' his voice dripped with sarcasm '—because I'm *livid—Your Highness*. Hell!' He swung away from her and raked a hand through his hair, 'I don't even know your name. Are you Rina, or Katarina?'

'I'm Kitty,' Kitty said quickly. 'It was my father's nickname for me when I was a little girl, and it stuck.' She risked another glance at him and felt her stomach dip. He was even more gorgeous than she remembered. In a pale grey suit and blue shirt he looked remote and forbidding, every inch the sophisticated, urbane businessman who was at the top of his game. He had been in her mind constantly since he had made love to her on the night of the ball, and now she could not prevent herself from staring at him and greedily absorbing his stunning looks.

'I didn't trick you intentionally. You mistook me for a servant at the ball and it seemed easier to go along with it. Be honest, would you have believed me if I'd told you my real identity?' she demanded when he glared at her. 'Everyone at the ball compared me unfavourably with my sister Liss, and they were right, I didn't look like a glamorous princess, I looked like the frumpy waitress you believed me to be. When we met on the beach later that night I was amazed when you said you found me attractive. You made me feel beautiful, even though I know I'm not,' she said bleakly, 'and I wanted to carry on being sexy Rina, rather than drab Kitty.'

'And having fooled me that you were Rina the waitress, you decided that it was a good opportunity to lose your virginity to an experienced man rather than a fumbling boy?' Nikos reminded her of her words when he had discovered her innocence, no hint of softening on his hard face. 'You are an heir to the crown of Aristo—*what the hell were you thinking of*?' he exploded furiously.

'It was a moment of madness,' Kitty defended herself. She moved her hand instinctively to her stomach, thinking of the tiny life that was growing inside her. 'I never dreamed that it would have such catastrophic consequences.'

'But it did, and now we must deal with those consequences,' Nikos told her bluntly. He paused and in the tense silence Kitty felt the same sickening dread that had filled her when, despite her fear of heights, she had volunteered to do a bungee jump for charity and had crouched at the top of the platform one hundred and fifty feet above the ground, preparing to launch herself over the edge.

'The only possible solution is for us to marry.'

There was no other alternative, Nikos acknowledged silently as he watched Kitty's mouth fall open in an expression of utter shock. He had vowed never to marry again, but if he wanted this child—and he did, unquestionably—then he would have to sacrifice his freedom and take a woman who had proved herself to be untrustworthy as his bride. 'It may not be ideal,' he snapped when Kitty shook her head frantically. 'Believe me, the situation is not what I would have chosen, either. But I have promised Sebastian that I will do my duty by you.'

The room suddenly seemed to be spinning—or was it her? Kitty collapsed back against the cushions. 'The idea is ridiculous,' she said faintly, repelled by the word 'duty'.

'Are you saying you have a better suggestion?' Nikos strolled over to the sofa and stared down at her, his eyebrows raised in an expression of haughty arrogance. 'I'm intrigued, Your Highness. What are you intending to do? I'd like to make it crystal clear, by the way, that no child of mine will be born illegitimately,' he added harshly when she stared at him in numb silence. 'And I should point out that Sebastian looked mightily relieved when I assured him of my intention to marry you as soon as it can be arranged. He has enough problems at the moment without worrying about you.'

'He doesn't need to worry about me. I can take care of myself,' Kitty muttered stubbornly, knowing in her heart that Sebastian's concern was not simply for her, but for the damaging effect her unplanned pregnancy might have on the monarchy. The situation was unprecedented. The people of Aristo were ardent royalists, but they would be dismayed to hear that a member of the royal family was pregnant and unmarried, and, as Nikos had said, this was a difficult enough time for Sebastian, the would-be-King who was waiting to be crowned.

But marry Nikos? Marry a man who was furious with her for lying to him, and who was staring at her with scathing contempt, as if she were the lowest life-form on the planet? It wasn't just ridiculous, it was utter madness and she absolutely would not agree to it. Since she was a little girl she had clung to the belief that she would one day fall in love and be loved in return, and she could not bear to see the fairy tale turn to ashes before her eyes. 'How can we marry?' she asked huskily. 'We don't love each other.'

Nikos spared her a derisive glance. 'What is love other than an illusion found in books and films?' he said sardonically. 'Too often people mistake *lust* for love, but it's not an error I'm ever likely to make. I am suggesting a marriage of convenience purely for the sake of our child.

'I have never known the identity of my father,' he revealed harshly. 'My mother would never tell me his name, but I have always wondered if I look like him or if we share similar traits.' He stared down at Kitty, his eyes suddenly blazing. 'I won't allow my child to suffer the trauma of not knowing his bloodline.'

Kitty was startled by the raw emotion in his voice, and even more shocked by the realisation that he was deadly serious. 'Nikos, let's be sensible about this,' she said desperately. 'I'm only three weeks pregnant and it would be madness to rush into marriage, and…and then find that it had been needless.' Her voice faltered when she imagined losing her baby. Already she had formed an emotional bond with the tiny new life that she and Nikos had unwittingly created, but she had to be prosaic. There was no history of miscarriages in her family but no one could foretell the future.

'There are plenty of other options open to us,' she went on when his jaw tightened. 'If you really want to play a part in the baby's life we could come to an arrangement about access and so on. You could visit the palace regularly…' She could feel his dark eyes boring into her and faltered. 'What I'm trying to say is that there is no need for either of us to make rash decisions. I'm not a poorly paid waitress, I have financial security and a supportive family here on Aristo, and I will manage to bring up this child perfectly well on my own.'

Nikos's blood had frozen at the word access, and it hit him suddenly that if he wasn't careful things could go very wrong. From the sound of it Kitty was determined to bring up their child on her own, but he was equally determined to be part of his baby's life. He was going to be a proper father, not some semi-stranger who visited the palace occasionally according to the rules of his visitation rights. Kitty had stated that she did not need him, and she certainly had the means to bring up a child without his help. Somehow he was going to have to convince her that he was indispensable—and he was prepared to use emotional blackmail to persuade her to marry him.

'So, are you going to tell your mother, while she is unwell and still grief-stricken by the death of the king, that you refuse to marry the father of your baby—and that you don't care that your actions will bring shame on the royal family?' he asked Kitty harshly. 'Sebastian is speaking to the queen now. He was anxious that she should learn of your pregnancy from him, rather than overhear the gossip among the servants which is inevitable after the scene in the drawing room.' His dark eyes bored into Kitty remorselessly when she gave a cry of distress. 'We can only hope that none of the guests or members of the press who were at the reception today actually guessed that you are pregnant. If we marry quickly no one need know that it's a shotgun wedding.'

He watched Kitty twisting her hands in the folds of her blue satin gown that the Queen and princesses customarily wore on formal state occasions. The floor-length dress disguised her shape, but beneath the stiff material he could picture the rounded fullness of her breasts and the dip and curve of her waist and hips, and he felt the familiar tug of sexual frustration that had plagued him since the night of the ball. He felt a sudden urge to pull the pins from her hair and run his fingers through the rich chestnut silk, and when she lifted her head he noted that her eyes were a deep, dark brown, velvet soft and fringed by impossibly long, thick lashes.

'Where are your glasses? Or were they part of your costume for your little theatrical performance the night we met?' he queried mockingly, forcing himself to move away from the temptation of her lush pink mouth. He was infuriated that he still wanted her despite the evidence that she had lied to him. The whole 'Rina the waitress' charade was still beyond his comprehension and he hated the idea that she had played him for a fool, but he couldn't forget the wild passion they had shared in the cave, and he was aware from the familiar tightening in his gut that his body was impatient for a repeat performance.

'I'm wearing my contact lenses today,' Kitty told him stiffly, 'and I've already explained that I didn't deliberately set out to trick you. Circumstances just…happened.' Her voice wavered as she tried to imagine her mother's shock and concern at the news of her pregnancy. Queen Tia would want her to marry Nikos, she acknowledged heavily, and Sebastian would be in favour of a quick solution to the embarrassing problem of her pregnancy. But how could she go through with it, and marry a man who had made it clear that he did not believe in love and would never care for her?

'Make no mistake, Kitty,' Nikos said quietly as he watched the play of emotions on her face. 'If you think I will simply walk away and allow you to bring up our child on your own, be warned, I will fight you for custody. Even if it means sacrificing my friendship with Sebastian I will have no compunction about dragging you and the rest of the royal family through the courts, and the fallout is likely to be extremely damaging to the monarchy.'

There was no doubt that Nikos was deadly serious, and a shiver ran through Kitty when she met his hard stare. The first time she had met him she had detected a ruthless side to him that he hid beneath a veneer of seductive charm. There was no sign of that charm now. He had called himself a pirate, and she realised with terrifying certainty that if she chose to do battle with him, she would lose.

'I am utterly determined that my child will live in Greece with me,' he said curtly. 'It's up to you if you want to take an active role in his upbringing.'

'What do you mean—an active role in his upbringing? It's my baby! And why do you think it's a boy? There's just as much chance it's a girl,' Kitty said shakily, still reeling from Nikos's assertion that he wanted their child to live in Greece. 'You can't possibly expect me to leave Aristo. I've lived here all my life.'

On the night of the ball the palace had seemed stifling, and she had felt a restless longing to escape the confines of royal life. Now that life seemed safe and reassuring and she wanted it to remain unchanged. But of course her life would change, she was going to be a mother, and in her heart she knew she could not remain at the palace and bring up her child without its father. 'If we were to marry, why couldn't you live here at the palace too?' she asked Nikos faintly.

'My business is based in Athens, and I need to be there,' he explained coolly. 'Naturally, as my wife, you will live with me, and although we will retain strong ties with Aristo and the royal family, our child, boy or girl,' he said pointedly, 'will grow up in Greece. I've discussed it with Sebastian and he is in complete agreement,' he added, as if that settled the matter.

Kitty shivered at the grim finality of his words. Sebastian had agreed, and, although her brother would never force her into marrying Nikos, she knew realistically that she had no option. She felt as though prison bars were closing around her. The room suddenly seemed claustrophobic and she stumbled to her feet and hurried across to the door. For the sake of her child, and the royal family, she would have to marry Nikos, but the prospect of being trapped in a loveless union with a man whose scathing opinion of marriage was well known, and who was furious with her for making a fool of him, filled her with despair.

'I need some time to think,' she muttered, every muscle in her body tensing when Nikos moved with the speed and grace of a big cat to stand in front of her.

'Far from being the poorly educated waitress you led me to believe at the ball, I have learned from Sebastian that you are a brilliant academic, and I have no doubt that you understand the gravity of the situation,' he said harshly. 'You have to make a decision *now*. Sebastian and your mother know that I am at this moment asking you to marry me, and we are expected to go immediately to the queen's private quarters and tell them your answer.

'As I see it, neither of us has any option,' he continued when she made no reply, and, although her mind screamed in silent rejection of his words, Kitty acknowledged with a leaden heart that he was right.

Warily she lifted her eyes to him, and even in the midst of her turmoil heat flared inside her when she studied his hard-boned, handsome face. It seemed a lifetime ago that they had made love in the cave, and when she focused on the cruel line of his mouth it seemed impossible that he had once kissed her with fierce passion. His aura of power was tangible, and she suddenly felt weak and drained. Everything was stacked in his favour, and she did not have the strength to fight him.

'When?' She forced the word past her numb lips, barely able to believe that she was contemplating agreeing to his offer. 'I suppose the wedding will have to be in the next few months?' Before she grew big with his child and everyone guessed the real reason for their marriage.

'Sooner than that,' Nikos corrected her. 'Sebastian has pencilled the eleventh of July into his diary, and cancelled all other state events.'

Kitty did a hurried mental calculation. 'That's three weeks from now!' Panic engulfed her and she shook her head wildly. 'I can't go through with it, Nikos.'

'Yes, you can,' he told her grimly, the cold determination in his eyes freezing her blood, 'because to be frank, Kitty, you have no choice.'

CHAPTER SEVEN

THE following three weeks passed in a blur, and Kitty felt increasingly detached from her life and the preparations for the wedding that were going on around her. She could almost believe she was caught up in a dream, and fully expected to wake up and find that she had never met a man called Nikos Angelaki, let alone become pregnant with his baby. But when she opened her eyes on the morning of her wedding and saw her bridal gown hanging against the wardrobe she was forced to make a reality check. This was real; in a few hours from now she would be his wife, and for the sake of the child developing inside her she could not escape the fate that awaited her.

'I told you all brides look beautiful on their wedding day,' Liss said later as she smoothed a crease from the full skirt of Kitty's white silk wedding dress. 'You look breathtaking. The dress shows off your figure perfectly. Don't you dare go back to wearing those ghastly, shapeless sweat-shirts you're so fond of! Not that Nikos will allow you to,' Liss added breezily. 'He leads a hectic social life and I bet he'll insist on buying you loads of gorgeous, sexy clothes for all the parties you'll be going to in Greece.'

Kitty felt a heavy weight settle around her heart as she contemplated her future life away from Aristo. 'You know I don't like parties,' she said dismally. 'In a few months from now I'll be huge, and I definitely won't look sexy—just fat. I've already gained weight, especially on my bust. Do you think I'm showing too much cleavage?' she asked worriedly, studying the dress's exquisite bodice, beaded with tiny pearls and crystals, and the firm swell of her breasts that appeared in imminent danger of spilling over the sweetheart neckline.

'Nikos's eyes will be on stalks,' Liss assured her cheerfully. 'I'm glad you decided to wear your hair down. It's a much softer style than when you pull it back off your face.'

'I suppose so, but it's not very practical.' Kitty's silky, dark chestnut hair was naturally wavy and it rippled down her back almost to her waist. At Liss's persuasion she had left it loose, and instead of a tiara and veil she had chosen a circlet of white roses for her headdress. Her sister had insisted on doing her make-up, but had kept it light, emphasising her brown eyes with a taupe shadow and adding a rose-pink gloss to her lips.

The finished effect was startling, and Kitty couldn't quite believe the woman in the mirror was her. Because of one night, and a few moments of uncharacteristic madness, her life had changed for ever. Her hand moved instinctively to her stomach, and she took a deep breath. She was marrying Nikos for the same reason that he was marrying her—for the sake of the child they had created—and there was no point in feeling emotional or fooled by the romance of the occasion.

'You're not supposed to look *practical*,' Liss argued, casting her eyes heavenwards. 'This is your wedding day, you're about to marry one of the sexiest men on the planet, *and* he sent you these… Gaea,' she called to the maid, 'bring in the flowers Mr Angelaki sent.'

The maid hurried out to the corridor and reappeared carrying an exquisite bouquet of pink and white rosebuds mixed with delicate fronds of gypsophila, which she handed to Kitty.

'I know you keep telling me this is a marriage of convenience, but there's obviously something between you and Nikos,' Liss said archly. 'I saw the glances he kept giving you at dinner last night—as if he couldn't wait to take you to bed.' Her eyes gleamed with amusement when Kitty blushed scarlet. 'And he phoned me from New

York a few days ago to ask my advice on your favourite flowers.'

'Did he?' Kitty strove to sound casual and told herself not to read too much into Liss's words, but her heart gave a little lurch when she buried her face in the blooms and inhaled their delicate perfume. No man had ever sent her flowers before, and the fact that Nikos had gone to some effort to ensure she had a bridal bouquet filled her with hope that this marriage was not as doomed to failure as she'd convinced herself. The roses were a talisman of hope, and tears glistened in her eyes when she stared at her reflection again and saw that Liss wasn't lying, and that by some miracle she really did look beautiful.

'Thank you for helping me with my dress,' she murmured. 'You know I'm hopeless with clothes, but thanks to your advice, and the designer's skill, my wedding dress is everything I could have hoped for.'

'No problem.' Liss shrugged her shoulders and gave a cursory glance in the mirror at her pale pink silk bridesmaid dress. 'I can't wait for everyone's reaction when they see you,' she said with a wide smile, 'especially Nikos's.'

Her smile faded when she glimpsed Kitty's over-bright eyes. 'I hope it works out for you,' Liss said softly. 'I know the baby was unplanned, and you've been pushed into getting married. I detect that Nikos is just as high-handed and determined to have his own way as Sebastian, and between the two of them, and the queen's stipulation that duty comes before everything, I bet you didn't stand a chance of refusing. But you must know that Seb and Mama and the rest of the family have your best interests at heart, and I'm sure that marrying Nikos is the right thing for you to do.'

'I hope so,' Kitty replied, unable to disguise the tremor in her voice. In the three weeks since their engagement had been announced to the media Nikos had only visited the palace twice before he had flown to America, and on both occasions they had spent no time alone. He had been polite and charming, and had completely won over Queen Tia, but to Kitty he had seemed remote and unapproachable and she hadn't known how to talk to him. Even when he had phoned from the States, their conversations had been limited to how she was feeling in the first stages of her pregnancy, and whether she was eating enough.

She had been able to reassure him on that point, Kitty thought gloomily. Apart from a couple of mornings when she'd felt nauseous, she was fit and healthy and had an appetite like a horse. Her mother said she was obviously one of those women who looked pregnant from early on, and that she was blooming, but she wasn't sure what Nikos's reaction would be to her body that was already filling out with his child.

More to the point, was he even going to see her body? she wondered. The wild passion they had shared in the cave seemed like a distant dream, and if it weren't for the fact that she was carrying his child she could almost believe she had imagined the pleasure of his mouth on hers and the touch of his hands on her breasts.

Would Nikos expect her to share his bed tonight—their wedding night? Kitty stared at her reflection as her face flooded with colour, and beneath her dress her breasts suddenly felt full and heavy. They had not discussed that aspect of their marriage, but Nikos was a supremely virile male and she guessed he would not want to live a life without sex. But he had given no indication, either on the day he had asked her to marry him, or the occasions she had seen him since, that he still desired her.

There had been virtually no physical contact between them since the one time he had made love to her. Even when they had posed for the official photographs to mark their engagement, Nikos had pressed his lips lightly to her hand, but hadn't kissed her properly on the mouth as she had longed for him to do. And when a member of the press had asked if he was in love, he had replied with some flippant remark that had made the journalists laugh but had emphasised to Kitty that she meant nothing to him.

Liss glanced at the clock. 'We'd better go. Are you ready?'

Was she? How ready could you be when you were about to leap into the unknown? Kitty took a deep breath and nodded. 'As ready as I'll ever be,' she murmured. Her heart was beating painfully fast when she walked over to the door, and as she turned and glanced around the room that had been her bedroom for twenty-six years she felt a sharp pang of sadness that after today the palace would no longer be her home. From now on home would be Athens, with Nikos, and she could only pray that her decision to marry him was the right one.

The private chapel in the grounds of the palace was packed with guests. When Kitty stepped through the arched doorway a murmur of excited voices seemed to echo around the nave, heads turned and she was conscious of the faint gasp that rippled through the crowd as they caught sight of her in her bridal gown. But her eyes were fixed straight ahead, on the tall, broad-shouldered man in a charcoal-grey suit who was standing at the altar.

Nikos must have known from the reaction of the guests that she had arrived, but he remained unmoving and did not even give a cursory glance over his shoulder towards his bride. His lack of curiosity, and his obvious reluctance to face the woman he felt obliged to marry, hit Kitty as painfully as if he had physically struck her, and trepidation knotted in her stomach. For a moment blind panic swept through her, and she could not restrain a shiver as she faced the reality of what she was about to do.

'Are you all right?' Sebastian whispered as he linked his arm with hers and stared down at her paper-white face. '*Theos,* Kitty, you're not going to faint, are you?'

The deep, pure notes of the organ music swirled up to the roof of the chapel and seemed to resound through Kitty's body. She stumbled, and for a few seconds the urge to turn and flee from the church, from Nikos, and the loveless future that awaited her, was overwhelming. But then she saw the anxiety in her brother's eyes, and the lesson that had been ingrained in her throughout her life—that adherence to duty was paramount—came to her rescue. She gripped her bouquet of roses and forced a smile for Sebastian, trying to disguise the fact that she felt as cold as if she had been carved from ice. 'I'm fine,' she assured him.

The journey down the aisle seemed to take for ever and when she finally reached Nikos's side she lifted her eyes warily to him and met his expressionless gaze. He made his responses in a cool, clear tone devoid of any emotion, but the constriction in Kitty's throat meant that her voice emerged as little more than a whisper, and she felt a deep sense of sadness that they had both lied when they had vowed to love and honour each other until death parted them. Tears stung her eyes when he slid a plain gold band onto her finger, and she could not stifle a shocked gasp when he followed her wedding ring with a spectacular diamond cluster that sparkled like teardrops in the sunlight that streamed down on them through the high windows.

When the priest murmured that Nikos could kiss his bride, Kitty turned her head, expecting a perfunctory brush of his lips, but as she lifted her face to him she was startled by the sudden blaze of heat in his eyes. Her heart thudded erratically in her chest when he drew her into his arms and she felt his strong, hard body pressed against hers. To her amazement he was no longer cold and remote, and she made no attempt to deny him when he lowered his head and claimed her mouth with undisguised hunger.

She had been starved of him for so long that she was unable to control her response to him. She kissed him back with equal fervour, welcoming the masterful sweep of his tongue between her lips and feeling a quiver of sexual excitement run through her at his low growl of frustration when the priest's polite cough reminded them that their display of passion was being watched by two hundred guests.

Their marriage was one of convenience, and a far cry from the love match she had dreamed of, Kitty acknowledged when they walked together back down the aisle and stepped out of the chapel into the bright sunshine. But for better or worse she was Nikos Angelaki's, wife and it was time she banished her romantic fantasies and accepted that she had married a man who would never love her but, for now at least it seemed, desired her.

'You look beautiful in your wedding dress,' he startled her by saying later at the reception, when the wedding lunch, speeches and champagne toasts were finally finished, and she had told him that she was going to get changed before they left for Athens. 'Don't take too long, *agape*. It will be another hour at least before we make it onto the helicopter and early evening by the time we land in Athens, and I am impatient to be alone with my bride.'

The sultry gleam in Nikos's eyes filled Kitty with nervous apprehension, and she hurried up to her room to change into her going-away outfit, desperate to spend a few minutes away from his disturbing presence. The jade silk skirt and close-fitting jacket had been Liss's choice that made the most of her curvy figure, and suited her colouring. As she studied her reflection she wondered if Nikos would approve when he discovered that she was wearing nothing beneath her suit other than a black lace bra and matching French knickers. From the sound of it he wanted their marriage to be a proper one, and she could not deny that the sexual chemistry between them was as strong as it had been on the night of the royal ball. But despite her desperate awareness of him, she felt nervous at the prospect of sharing his bed when she barely knew him. For her, the intimacy of making love was a big issue, but she had a feeling that Nikos regarded sex as the single benefit of their enforced marriage.

Lost in her thoughts she walked back down the corridor, but as she turned the corner she cannoned into Vasilis Sarondakos, and her heart sank.

'You hardly look the joyful bride,' he said mockingly. 'What's the matter, Kitty? Are you afraid that if you leave your husband alone for too long his attention will stray—towards your sister perhaps?'

Vasilis was drunk. His speech was slurred, and Kitty wrinkled her nose when she caught a waft of alcohol on his breath. She had been dismayed to find his name on the guest list, but he was an old family friend, and she'd reminded herself that after today she would probably never see him again. She attempted to push past him, but he grabbed her arm and shoved her up against the wall. *'Let go of me!'* She tried to jerk free of his hold but Vasilis tightened his grip and laughed.

'You have every reason to worry,' he taunted. 'Liss was blessed with more than her fair share of good looks, and Nikos is a notorious playboy.'

'Shut up, Vasilis!' Kitty couldn't quite banish her envy of her sister's beauty, and she despised herself. 'There's nothing going on between Liss and Nikos. He married me, didn't he?'

'Ah, but the reason for your hasty trip down the aisle isn't as secret as you might wish,' Vasilis said with a sly wink. 'But I've got to hand it to Angelaki—he's even more of a ruthless social climber than I realised, and he struck gold with you. Who else would have set out to deliberately seduce a naïve, virgin princess, impregnate her with his child and then marry her pronto to spare embarrassment to the royal family? I'm surprised Sebastian hasn't knighted him for services above and beyond the call of duty,' Vasilis finished bitterly.

'Don't be ridiculous,' Kitty said faintly, reeling from Vasilis's shocking statement. How on earth did he know about her pregnancy? 'What do you mean when you say Nikos is a social climber?' she demanded. 'He's a multimillionaire who heads his own hugely successful company.'

'A company that he inherited after he seduced

another gullible woman,' Vasilis said sneeringly. 'It's not only Hollywood starlets who sleep their way to the top. Nikos Angelaki was the illegitimate son of a peasant woman. He grew up in the slums of Athens, and as a teenager he was already involved with the criminal underworld.' Vasilis paused when he saw Kitty's shocked expression, and gave an unpleasant smile. 'I take it your new husband hasn't told you about his past? Ask him about the tattoo on his shoulder if you don't believe me.

'Somehow, Nikos met a millionairess, Larissa Petridis, daughter of the shipping magnate Stamos Petridis,' Vasilis continued. 'Larissa had inherited her father's company after his death. She was a spinster with a penchant for good-looking young men. Rumour has it that she quickly became besotted with charming, handsome Nikos, despite the fact that he was twenty years younger than her. Nikos seized his chance to escape a life of poverty and he became her lover, and when Larissa died a few years later she left Petridis Shipping to him. Not a bad prize for being a stud to a lonely older woman, was it?' Vasilis jeered.

Kitty felt dizzy as Vasilis's poisonous words swirled in her mind, but she was determined not to reveal her shock at his revelations by fainting, and she pressed her back against the wall for support. 'I don't believe you,' she muttered. 'How do you know so much about Nikos?'

'I hired someone to make a few enquiries,' Vasilis said without a flicker of shame. 'I like to discover the skeletons in people's closets. You never know when the information might come in useful. I'll show you the report my private eye filed on Angelaki if you like. It makes interesting reading. Almost as interesting as this week's edition of *Glamorous* magazine,' Vasilis added, grinning at Kitty's puzzled expression.

'Is there anything to *read* in a downmarket publication devoted entirely to celebrity gossip?' she queried coldly.

'Not much,' Vasilis admitted, 'but there are plenty of pictures showing what your new husband was getting up to in the three weeks prior to your wedding.'

'Nikos was in the US, working hard to tie up a business deal,' Kitty said sharply.

'Well, he was certainly working hard, but in the bedroom rather than the boardroom. Face it, Kitty,' Vasilis said nastily. 'You're not Angelaki's type—which I guess is why he spent the last weeks with his mistress, Shannon Marsh…here's the evidence.' He withdrew a copy of the glossy magazine from his jacket pocket and flipped it open to a double page spread of photographs showing Nikos and a stunning, tanned blonde.

In the photos Nikos looked bronzed and gorgeous with a lock of his dark hair falling across his brow. He was relaxed and laughing with his beautiful companion and the obvious familiarity between them tore at Kitty's heart even more than the images of Shannon pressing her naked breasts against Nikos's muscular chest.

She snatched the magazine from Vasilis and scanned the short paragraph beneath the photos, paling when her own name leapt from the page together with the speculation that, while Nikos was about to marry a European princess, he was still clearly smitten with his American lover.

'I told you that you should have married me.' Vasilis swayed unsteadily. 'I wouldn't have humiliated you on your wedding day. As it is, many of the guests here today have probably read this over their breakfast this morning, and there's fevered speculation among them about the real reason why Nikos hurried you down the aisle.'

A wave of nausea swept over Kitty at Vasilis's words and her fragile self-confidence shattered. The wedding guests hadn't stared at her in the chapel because she'd been transformed into a beautiful bride—they had been comparing her to Shannon Marsh, whose stunning figure was revealed in all its lissom glory in a magazine that had worldwide circulation.

And what about Nikos, and his apparent

eagerness to take her to bed—how could he possibly desire her when he had Shannon waiting for him in America? She would be a poor consolation prize, Kitty thought miserably.

She jerked out of Vasilis's hold, and felt no sympathy when he stumbled drunkenly. She was shocked to realise that her whole body was shaking with reaction. The tension wouldn't be good for the baby, and the knowledge forced her to take a ragged breath. The baby was the only thing that mattered, the only reason she had married Nikos, and from now on she would concentrate all her energies on the tiny scrap of life growing inside her.

'Angelaki only married you for the kudos of having a royal bride.'

Vasilis's spiteful taunt followed Kitty as she walked slowly back down the stairs, but she did not pause or look back. She knew exactly why Nikos had made her his wife. He wanted his child. But he had told her once that he valued his freedom above everything, and the magazine photos were clear evidence that he had no intention of taking his marriage vows seriously.

CHAPTER EIGHT

KITTY had been taught from an early age that members of the royal family never displayed their emotions in public, and the training proved invaluable for the remainder of the reception. Somehow she managed to smile at the well-wishers who crowded onto the palace lawn where Nikos's helicopter was waiting, and she was confident she had fooled Sebastian and the queen that she was happy to be leaving Aristo for her new life in Greece.

As soon as the helicopter took off she closed her eyes and feigned sleep, unable to face Nikos. She reminded herself that in the days before their wedding he had been free to do as he chose—even if that meant cavorting on a public beach with his half-naked lover—but she felt deeply humiliated that he had flaunted his affair so openly.

As for Vasilis's story about Nikos's past—she did not know what to think. Knowing Vasilis's warped personality as she did, it was entirely likely that he had employed an investigator to dig up any dirt on Nikos, and she supposed the facts would be easy to verify. She did not care if Nikos came from a poor background, but the idea that he had acquired his wealth and success because he had played on the emotions of a rich older woman filled her with dismay.

Her thoughts tormented her as the helicopter flew over the sea, and her heart ached as Aristo faded to a tiny speck in the distance. Nikos had been speaking to the pilot, but now he came and sat down next to her, and despite everything she had learned of him her senses quivered at his nearness. She felt his gaze on her and squeezed her eyes tightly shut. Tension gripped her but after a few moments she heard him sigh, and when she peeped at him she saw he was engrossed in his newspaper.

Nikos lived in the heart of Athens in an imposing tower block that loomed high above the busy city streets. It was a far cry from the peace and tranquillity of Aristo, and Kitty felt a pang of homesickness when his chauffeur-driven limousine turned into the underground car park beneath his apartment.

'When I am at work my driver, Stavros, will take you to wherever you wish to go. He is a trained bodyguard and you are not to leave the apartment without him,' Nikos told her when they stepped into the lift.

'I didn't have a bodyguard on Aristo and I won't need one here,' Kitty argued, startled.

'It's different on Aristo. All the members of the royal family are well loved by the Aristan people, and no one would ever harm you there. But here in Athens you are already something of a talking point,' Nikos said tersely. 'People, especially the press, are fascinated by the idea of having a princess in their midst. You can't have missed the paparazzi who tailed us from the airport. Your photograph will be on the front pages of all tomorrow's papers, and unfortunately that level of interest isn't always healthy.'

Kitty frowned. 'What do you mean?'

'I mean that there are some individuals who resent my wealth, and yours,' he told her grimly. 'I don't wish to scare you, Kitty, but you have to be aware of the possibility of kidnap—a possibility that is reduced to zero if you do as you are told and always stay close to Stavros.'

He had instructed Stavros to tail her every move, but not only to ensure her safety, Nikos brooded. Kitty had insisted she wanted the baby, but he was taking no chances—he would know her whereabouts every minute of the day.

The expression on Nikos's face warned Kitty to say no more on the subject of a bodyguard, but her heart sank. She had thought she would have more freedom here in Athens, away from the stiff protocol of palace life, but it seemed that she had swapped one prison for another, and she was to have her own personal jailer.

The lift halted at the top floor, and Nikos took her by surprise when he swept her into his arms and carried her into his apartment. 'Now you are truly my bride,' he murmured, frowning slightly when he noted how she had stiffened at his touch.

His words settled like concrete in Kitty's stomach as she wondered if he was intending to carry her on into his bedroom and make her his wife in the time-honoured fashion. She could not forget the magazine pictures of him and Shannon Marsh, and she wriggled in his arms so that he was forced to set her on her feet. 'I'm too heavy for you,' she muttered. 'I'll break your back.'

'I think that is unlikely, *agape,*' he drawled, his eyes narrowing when she refused to meet his gaze. It was the first time she had visited his home, and it was perhaps natural that she seemed tense, Nikos told himself. And of course she wasn't merely visiting, this would be her home too now, and it must seem very different from what she was used to. His penthouse apartment was luxurious but it was not a royal palace.

They would both have to make adjustments, he acknowledged. He liked his space, and since his divorce had never invited any of his lovers to spend a night at the apartment. Now Kitty would be living here; but she was his wife, not his mistress, and he could not expect their relationship to only be confined to the bedroom. Presumably they would eat breakfast together every morning, and dine together when he returned home in the evening, and he wasn't sure how he felt about sharing his private domain. He had been alone for so long that it had become his way of life, but in a few months from now the baby would be here, and he felt a fierce jolt of excitement as he imagined life with his child.

He would be a good father, he vowed silently. His child would want for nothing, especially his love. But for the sake of the child he would have to help Kitty settle in Athens so that she was not tempted to flee back to Aristo. He glanced at her, his eyes narrowing on the firm swell of her breasts outlined beneath her silk jacket. The matching skirt moulded her delightfully round bottom, and as he imagined tugging the jade silk over her hips he felt himself harden, and he was fiercely tempted to lead her down the hall to the master bedroom and demonstrate that from now on the only place she would ever want to be was in Athens—in his bed.

His heartbeat quickened and he placed his hand on her shoulder, stroking back her long chestnut hair that felt like silk against his skin. He wanted to brush her hair to one side and press his lips to the pulse beating at the base of her throat, but once again he was aware of her sudden tension and he dropped his hand back to his side.

He did not know what was wrong with her, and, quite frankly, he wasn't in the mood to play games. When he had kissed her in the church her eager response had been a satisfactory indication that she shared his impatience to consummate their marriage. But since then she had cooled considerably, and her edginess puzzled him. Maybe she just needed time to adjust? Marriage, impending motherhood and moving from Aristo to Athens were all momentous changes to her life, and he guessed that she had found the wedding a strain. Even though they had planned to keep it low-key, the marriage of a member of the royal family was a significant event and it had seemed as though half the population of Aristo had been invited to the wedding.

Curbing his impatience to take her to bed, he moved away from her. 'I'll give you a guided tour of the apartment, and perhaps you'll start to feel more at home.'

'Thank you.' Kitty followed Nikos down the hall, her heart sinking as she glanced around. His apartment was ultra-modern and minimalist with white marble floors and pale walls teamed with black leather sofas and silver furnishings. It was a typical bachelor pad designed for a busy executive and not the sort of place she could imagine bringing up a baby. She remembered the shabby but comfortable palace nursery where she had spent her childhood: toys strewn across the floor and the vast bookshelf stuffed with her beloved fairy tales. Tears welled in her eyes when she recalled how her father had visited the nursery every evening to read to her, even if he'd had to interrupt important meetings to do so. She couldn't imagine Nikos doing the same for their child, and she could not picture them living here together, playing happy families.

'There will be no need for you to spend much time in here,' he informed her when he ushered her into the gleaming, stainless-steel kitchen. 'My butler and cook, Sotiri, takes care of everything on the domestic front. I'll introduce you to him later.'

He continued on down the hall, past the elegant dining room, and three generous-sized bedrooms, one of which Kitty supposed would be a nursery when the baby was born. At the far end of the corridor Nikos flung open the remaining door—and Kitty came to an abrupt halt in the doorway.

The master bedroom overlooked the Acropolis which, now that dusk had fallen, was illuminated by spotlights and gleamed gold against the indigo sky. It was a breathtaking sight, but Kitty's attention was riveted by the enormous bed that dominated the room, with its leather headboard and black silk sheets. Floor-to-ceiling mirrors covered the length of one wall, reflecting the bed—and its occupants, she realised, her heart lurching when she spied the bottle of champagne cooling in an ice bucket. It was a room designed for seduction, and she wondered how many other women Nikos had brought here and whether they had paused to admire the view before they had joined him on that huge bed.

She stared at him, her heart hammering in her chest as she wondered if he was anticipating taking *her* to bed *right* now.

'The maid unpacked the trunks sent over from the palace and put your belongings in your dressing room. Come, I'll show you.' Nikos walked over to a door at the far end of the master bedroom, and Kitty hurried after him, grateful for the reprieve. The dressing room was spacious, fitted with oak wardrobes, a matching dressing table, and a large sofa, while another door led to the en suite bathroom. Slowly some of her panic receded when she realised that she would have a measure of privacy.

Nikos had opened the wardrobes and was studying their meagre contents with a frown. 'This can't be all your clothes. Why didn't you send everything over from Aristo?'

'That *is* everything,' Kitty said tightly. 'I've never taken much interest in fashion.'

'Well, I suggest you start.' He flicked impatiently through the hangers. 'I appreciate that you are still in mourning for your father, but your entire wardrobe seems to consist of black outfits.'

'They're not mourning clothes. I wear black because it makes me look slimmer.' Kitty could feel the stain of hot colour flood her cheeks at his scathing expression.

'Black doesn't suit you,' he stated bluntly, 'and I can see we need to go shopping. I do a lot of socialising, and my diary is already filling up with invitations from people who are all eager to meet my princess bride.'

Kitty's heart sank at his words, and she couldn't help thinking that the 'people' Nikos had mentioned were likely to be disappointed when they met her and discovered that she was not the glamorous, sophisticated royal they expected.

Nikos strolled over to her, and the butterflies in her stomach leapt into life once more when he took her hand in his and led her firmly through the connecting door, into the master bedroom. 'I approve of the outfit you are wearing now,' he murmured, his voice so deep and sensuous that Kitty could not prevent the tremor that ran through her, and she caught her breath when he slid his hand over her shoulder and down the front of her jacket.

'Liss chose it for me,' she mumbled.

He laughed softly, 'In that case it's a pity your sister did not choose all your clothes.'

At his words Kitty felt a familiar stab of jealousy. Liss was beautiful and glamorous, and she had exquisite taste in clothes. If she had been at the royal ball six weeks ago, Nikos would almost certainly have noticed her, and he would never have walked down to the beach and made love to a waitress called Rina.

All her old insecurities came flooding back. She hadn't needed Vasilis to tell her that she wasn't Nikos's type. She was only too aware that she did not have a model's figure like Liss, or Shannon Marsh, and she could not bear the idea of him comparing her plump curves with his American mistress's gorgeous, toned body.

Nikos had discarded his jacket, and her mouth went dry when he began to casually unbutton his shirt.

'I want to sleep alone tonight,' she told him baldly, her heart jerking painfully beneath her ribs. 'It's been a long day and I'm exhausted.' She felt as though she had been on an emotional roller coaster and now her limbs were trembling with reaction.

Nikos had stilled at her startling announcement, and now his brows rose quizzically. 'In that case why didn't you sleep on the journey here? Your rather childish pretence to be asleep didn't fool me for a second,' he added.

The note of impatience in his voice triggered Kitty's temper. It was all right for him. He had got his own way on everything. *Her* life had been turned upside down, but their marriage was barely going to have any impact on him at all.

'You're right; I did pretend to be asleep—so that I wouldn't have to talk to you,' she said wildly. 'And the very idea of going to bed with you makes me feel ill.'

Nikos's jaw tightened as he sought to control his anger. He had no patience for feminine wiles—or tantrums. 'That's not the impression you gave me when I kissed you in the church,' he said silkily. 'What has caused your sudden change of heart, I wonder?'

Kitty blushed as she remembered how she had responded to him. She had been blissfully unaware then that he had spent the days before their wedding with his American mistress. Nikos had ceased unbuttoning his shirt but it was open to the waist and her eyes were drawn to his broad, golden-skinned chest. He was so gorgeous, and she was so very ordinary, she thought miserably. The idea of undressing in front of him and exposing her body made her cringe.

'What's the real issue here, Kitty?' he demanded, frustrated by his inability to understand her.

It was clear from the determined set of his jaw that he was prepared to wait all night if necessary for an explanation. Kitty hesitated for a moment and then muttered, 'At the reception, when I went to change out of my wedding dress, I met someone—a family friend…' Her voice faltered at the idea of calling loathsome Vasilis Sarondakos a friend. 'I learned something about *you*,' she revealed hesitantly, 'facts about your background that I was unaware of, such as that you had grown up in poverty and been in trouble with the law.'

In the tense silence that stretched between them Kitty felt increasingly awkward, and she blurted out the doubts that Vasilis had planted in her mind. 'I also learned of the rumours that you owe your business success to a wealthy heiress, Larissa Petridis, who bequeathed you her father's shipping company when she died because you had been her toy-boy lover.'

'Who was this friend, I wonder?' Nikos drawled in a dangerously soft tone. His brows arched in an expression of arrogant amusement but the hard gleam in his eyes warned Kitty that he was furious, and she took an involuntary step backwards. 'At least have the decency to name the individual who has gone to such trouble to stab me in the back.'

Kitty hesitated. 'It was a friend of Sebastian's—Vasilis Sarondakos.'

Nikos gave a harsh laugh. 'Sarondakos is no

friend of your brother's. Sebastian only included him on the guest list because King Aegeus was good friends with Vasilis's father.'

That was the reason she had never told anyone about Vasilis's assault on her, Kitty thought bleakly. Vasilis had played on his family's royal connections for too long, but had he been lying about Nikos?

'Are the rumours true?' she asked in a choked voice.

'The details of my background are no secret.' Nikos gave a careless shrug. He appeared relaxed but Kitty sensed his simmering anger, and she took another step backwards until her legs hit the end of the bed and she had nowhere else to go.

'I grew up in the slums, in conditions you cannot imagine,' he told her harshly. 'How could *you* know—a princess who has spent her whole life in a royal palace enjoying the trappings of wealth and luxury? My mother worked all the hours she could to feed and clothe me, but she was young and poorly educated, forced to struggle alone after the man who had seduced her—my father—abandoned her, and her family disowned her when they learned she was pregnant.'

Nikos's face hardened. 'You have no idea what it is like to be hungry, to roam the streets like a stray dog and steal food to survive. I am not ashamed of my background, and the hunger in my belly fuelled my determination to make a better life for me and my mother. But it's true that there was a time in my late teens when I was drawn to the street gangs, and if it had not been for Larissa Petridis I could easily be in prison right now rather than the head of a multimillion pound company.'

Kitty stared at Nikos with wide, troubled eyes. 'So you did seduce a rich older woman and became her lover in the hope of inheriting her company?'

'My relationship with Larissa is not open for discussion,' Nikos said coldly. 'I admit I inherited Petridis Shipping from Larissa, but although she was an amazing person, she was an appalling businesswoman and when I took over the company it was on the verge of bankruptcy. I worked long and hard to turn it around, and I take all the credit for the fact that Petridis Angelaki Shipping has recently announced record profits.'

While he had been speaking Nikos had moved closer, and now Kitty realised that she was trapped between him and the bed. She could feel the anger emanating from him and, heart thumping, she edged sideways and gave a cry of alarm when his hand shot out and gripped her chin. *Let me go.*

'What's the matter, Kitty?' Nikos demanded grimly. 'Are you afraid you'll get your hands dirty if you touch me now you know I'm of peasant stock rather than a blue-blooded aristocrat?'

'Of course I don't think that,' she denied instantly. She didn't care about his social status, or where he came from—it was where he had been for the weeks leading up to their wedding and the woman he had spent his time with that bothered her.

'We should never have married,' she said wildly, her stomach churning at the images in her mind of him making love to Shannon. 'I should never have allowed myself to be talked into it…I want an annulment.'

'Because you think I'm not good enough for you?' he queried furiously. 'I know you are a princess but I had no idea that you are also a spoilt, over-indulged snob.'

'That's not the reason,' she snapped, stung by his scathing tone. She reached into her handbag for the magazine that Vasilis had given her, all the anger and misery that had been building inside her for the past few hours exploding in a torrent of emotion. 'You've made a fool of me, Nikos—not just here in Greece, but everywhere. *Glamorous* magazine has a worldwide circulation and everyone, including most of the guests at our wedding, will have seen *these*…' She hurled the magazine at him, open at the page of the damning photos. 'Everyone must have been laughing at me behind my back—fat, frumpy Kitty whose new husband spent the weeks preceding the wedding flaunting his affair with his beautiful blonde mistress.

'No wonder there's widespread speculation about the real reason you married me. Most people will have put two and two together and realised I'm pregnant. Like me, everyone who has seen those pictures will know you never had any intention of being a faithful husband.'

Kitty took a deep, shuddering breath, shocked to realise that her whole body was trembling and her heart was beating so hard that she could feel it slamming beneath her ribs. It couldn't be good for the baby. She placed a hand protectively on her stomach and her fury drained away as a wave of nausea swept over her. She could hear a peculiar rushing noise in her ears and suddenly strong hands were on her shoulders, forcing her to sit down on the bed, and her head was pushed down towards her knees so that her blood rushed to her brain.

'Take a deep breath…and another.' Nikos's voice sounded harsh with impatience, and silly tears welled in Kitty's eyes and slid down her cheeks when he continued savagely, 'If you carry on like this you could lose the baby.'

'Maybe you'd be relieved if I did,' Kitty whispered. 'At least then we could end this façade of a marriage.'

He swore long and hard and leaned down so

that his face was level with hers. 'Accuse me of whatever else you like,' he said grittily, 'but never that. Our child was conceived by accident but I do not regret it, even if you do.'

'I don't—of course I don't,' she denied quickly, scrubbing her wet face with the back of her hand. 'And I know you want the baby—just as I know it's the only reason you married me.'

Nikos stared at her, his expression unfathomable. 'You almost passed out. I'm going to call the doctor.'

Kitty shook her head frantically. 'I don't need a doctor. I'm fine now, I was just upset—that's all.'

'About the photos?' Nikos glanced down at the copy of the magazine in his hands. 'Where did you get this? I'm surprised you read this sort of trash.'

'I don't usually. Vasilis gave it to me.' Kitty flushed beneath Nikos's hard stare. She felt horribly embarrassed by her loss of temper, and wished he would go away and leave her alone, but the determined gleam in his eyes warned her he was not going to let the matter drop. 'I knew you had flown to America after I'd agreed to marry you, but I would have preferred you to have been honest about your reasons for going,' she said stiffly. 'Obviously you didn't go on business, but to see your mistress, and you didn't even bother to be discreet about it,' she added bitterly. 'You've made me a laughing stock, Nikos, and I'll never forgive you.'

When he made no reply she lifted her head to find him studying the magazine photos intently— and probably comparing her to the gorgeous Shannon, she thought bleakly. He looked at her, and his dark eyes seemed to bore into her skull, as if he could divine her thoughts.

'It's true that I went to the US with the express intention of seeing Shannon,' he said steadily. 'We had enjoyed a relationship for several months before I met you. It was a casual affair; we both lead busy lives and we met up whenever we happened to be in the same country. But I owed it to her to end it face to face rather than by a long-distance phone call.'

Kitty's heart jerked at the words 'end it' but the photos still haunted her. 'In those pictures you and Shannon are rather more than *face to face*,' she said sarcastically. 'The two of you are practically naked and superglued together. I don't *care*—you understand,' she insisted sharply. 'I just hate the idea that our wedding guests felt sorry for me— Princess Plump who couldn't hold onto her man even before the trip down the aisle.'

'*Theos*, Kitty, why do you have such a low opinion of yourself?' Nikos growled impatiently. 'You have a fantastic body and you know damn well I can't keep my hands off you. If I'd had a better hold on my self-control the night we met, we might not be in this mess now,' he added tersely. 'These pictures are *old*.' He waved the magazine at her. 'They were taken several months ago, soon after Shannon and I had met, and at the height of our affair. When I visited her three weeks ago to tell her I was getting married, we met in New York. We were nowhere near the Caribbean beach shown in the photos.'

'But the article gives the impression that the pictures were taken recently,' Kitty said faintly, her head reeling.

Nikos shrugged. 'Of course. Publications like this print rubbish all the time, and unfortunately there's nothing to stop them from digging out archive photos. The written piece is careful not to suggest that it is actually referring to the pictures above it. I'll contact my lawyers and see if we can get an apology from the magazine, but to be honest I've learned to ignore the paparazzi and I suggest you do the same.'

That was easy for him to say—he hadn't been made to feel an idiot. But it seemed pointless to say so, and Kitty suddenly felt so drained that she could barely think straight. She could not bring herself to look at Nikos, and she gave a little start of surprise when he hunkered down beside her and slid his hand beneath her chin to tilt her face to his.

'I married you today with every intention of being a faithful husband,' he said with a quiet intensity that shook her. 'I admit I did not live the life of a monk before I met you, but now there is the baby to consider, and I will do my duty towards you and our child. Shannon is in my past,' he continued as Kitty tried to ignore the dull feeling inside her at his emphasis on the word 'duty'. 'You are my future, Kitty.'

His hand lay on her thigh, and seemed to burn her flesh through her silk skirt. He looked devastatingly sexy with his dark hair falling over his brow, and she was seriously tempted to place her hand on his bare chest and run her fingers through the dark hairs that arrowed down his flat abdomen and disappeared beneath the waistband of his trousers.

She knew he wanted to take her to bed, could see the feral hunger in his eyes and hear the sudden quickening of his breath. But did he want to make love to her because he desired her, or because he believed it was his right to have sex with his wife whom he had only married out of *duty*?

'But we're not like most newly married couples,' Kitty said carefully. 'We married because I'm pregnant, and I feel that we should wait a while before we—' she could feel her face burning beneath his sardonic stare '—before we have relations.'

'Can I take it that by "have relations" you mean, have sex?'

'We barely know each other,' Kitty snapped, stung by the mockery in his tone. In her agitation she jumped up from the bed, and he straightened up so that he towered over her.

'Agreed, but we will get to know each other a lot quicker if we share a bed,' Nikos said tersely.

'That isn't the "getting to know" I mean.' Kitty bit her lip, aware from his grim expression that Nikos's desire was rapidly turning to anger. 'In a few months from now we will be parents. Surely we should spend some time before the baby comes learning about each other's thoughts and feelings? There has to be more to our relationship than just sex.'

The flame that had warmed his eyes died, and now they were dark and icy cold. 'Actually there doesn't,' he told her harshly. 'Sexual awareness drew us together in the first place, and the child that was created as a result of our passion is the only other link between us.'

He saw the flash of hurt in her eyes, and for a fleeting second something tugged at his heart, but he instantly dismissed it. Kitty's suggestion of sharing their thoughts and feelings was his idea of hell. His thoughts were his own; he'd learned long ago, when he was growing up on the streets, to keep his own counsel and trust no one—and that lesson had been brutally reinforced by his ex-wife.

'We know we are sexually compatible,' he continued in a coldly clinical tone, 'and I believe that is as good a basis for marriage as any. The chemistry between us burns as fiercely now as it did on the night of the ball,' he insisted when she shook her head. 'But perhaps this will convince you.'

'Nikos…' He moved before she had time to react, and her cry of protest was lost when he snaked his arm around her waist and lowered his head to claim her mouth in a searing kiss. His lips were firm, moving over hers with fierce urgency, while his tongue probed the stubborn line of her mouth with an implacable determination to force her response.

And it was growing harder and harder to resist him. Crushed against his chest, Kitty could feel the heat that emanated from him, and smell his clean, male scent—a mixture of soap and aftershave and another, more subtle scent of male pheromones—that inflamed her senses. When he had kissed her in the church she had wanted him to never stop, and now she felt that same sense of being swept away to a place where nothing but Nikos and the mastery of his touch mattered. Her mind and body were locked in a battle where caution waged against the sensations he was arousing in her and she could feel her resolve slipping away.

He slid his hand beneath her hair and cupped her nape, angling her head so that he could deepen the kiss to something so flagrantly erotic that Kitty's will crumbled and she sagged against him, parting her mouth beneath his. She was barely aware of him unfastening her jacket and sliding it over her shoulders. And then somehow they were on the bed and he had removed her bra, and she gasped when he cupped her breasts in his palms and stroked his fingers lightly across her nipples, so that they swelled to tight, tingling peaks.

He was her husband; they were tied together because of the child they had created during a brief passionate encounter, and maybe he was right, maybe sex would be a start to them building a relationship. She was so confused by what she wanted, but the solid ridge of his arousal nudging her thigh drove the uncertainty from her mind and replaced it with piercing desire that caused molten heat to flood between her legs. She gave up trying to fight him and the dictates of her treacherous body, and curled her arms around his neck, but instead of responding to the tentative foray of her tongue into his mouth, Nikos lifted his head and stared down at her, his dark eyes glittering.

'Yes, the chemistry is still there, isn't it, *agape*?' he drawled, his mouth curving into a mocking smile when she blinked at him dazedly.

To her shocked disbelief he rolled off her and sauntered out of the room, leaving her lying half naked on the bed. He returned almost instantly with what looked like a pile of laundry in his hands.

'Sheets,' he told her. 'You'll need them if you're going to make up a bed on the sofa in your dressing room.' He paused and his eyes trailed an insolent path over her flushed cheeks and bare breasts where her nipples were still jutting provocatively. 'Unless you've changed your mind about wanting to sleep alone, of course?'

'I…' Kitty's tongue seemed to have cleaved to the roof of her mouth, and she felt sick with humiliation that she had succumbed so easily to his potent charm.

'Still not sure, I see.' Nikos laughed softly as he walked over to the bed, dropped the sheets into her lap and scooped her up into his arms, blithely ignoring her sharp cry of protest as her battered pride finally woke up. 'We both know that I could make love to you for the rest of the night, and you would be willing and responsive in my arms,' he told her with breathtaking arrogance that made her want to hit him, 'but I don't want a reluctant bride. I have never taken a woman against her will in my life, and I don't intend to start with you, *agape*.'

He strode though the connecting doors into her

dressing room and dumped her unceremoniously on the sofa. 'You know where to find me when you've admitted the truth to yourself.'

'The truth being that I find you irresistible, I suppose?' Kitty said grittily as she clutched the sheets to her breasts. She hated him, and hated herself more for her pathetic inability to resist him. 'You'll be waiting a long time.'

In reply he dropped a brief, stinging kiss on her lips that left her aching for more. 'I don't think so,' he said confidently. 'The sofa pulls out to a bed, by the way, and it's extremely comfortable. Sleep well, Kitty—' he turned back in the doorway and gave her another mocking smile as he murmured '—if you can.'

CHAPTER NINE

THE sofa bed was as comfortable as Nikos had promised, but Kitty tossed and turned beneath the sheets for most of the night as she fought the urge to bury her face in the pillows and cry. Nikos was so in control, and he made her feel so stupid. She didn't even know now why she had made such a fuss about sleeping with him; it was just some deeply ingrained instinct for self-protection that warned her against giving herself to a man who might be her husband, but was a man she knew very little about.

Eventually she fell into a fitful doze and when she woke sunlight was streaming through the blinds. She took her time showering and drying her hair, but she could not put off facing Nikos for ever, and, spurred on by hunger, and the knowledge that she must eat for the baby, she ventured out of her room.

She found him sitting at the breakfast table on the terrace, engrossed in his newspaper. Dressed in pale jeans and a cream shirt that contrasted with his bronzed skin, he was impossibly handsome, and Kitty halted in the living room while she tried to control her desperate awareness of him.

He stood up when she stepped onto the terrace, and pulled out a chair for her. She had steeled herself for a sarcastic enquiry about how she had slept, and she knew from the dark shadows beneath her eyes that he would guess she'd barely slept at all, but to her relief he made no comment about the previous night.

'There is fruit and yoghurt and fresh rolls, but if you would like something cooked I'll tell Sotiri,' he greeted her.

'This will be fine,' Kitty mumbled, glancing at the dish of mixed summer berries and the creamy yoghurt, 'but no coffee, thank you. I haven't been able to drink it since I fell pregnant.'

'Have you suffered much from morning sickness?'

'Not really—I've felt nauseous a few times, but unfortunately it hasn't affected my appetite. I'm already bursting out of most of my clothes.' She broke off, blushing furiously when Nikos's gaze hovered on her blouse that was too tight and was gaping over her breasts. 'No doubt I'll get a lot bigger yet,' she muttered dismally as she resisted pouring honey onto her yoghurt.

Nikos's eyes narrowed at her rueful tone, and he voiced the question that had been gnawing away at him. 'How do you feel about this baby, Kitty?'

'I don't know,' she replied slowly. 'To be honest, it all seems to be part of a dream and I keep thinking that one day soon I'll wake up and find I'm at the palace on Aristo with nothing to think about other than my research work for the museum.'

'Is that what you wish?'

'I would be lying if I didn't say that part of me wishes I was back there,' she admitted. 'Aristo was my home for my whole life and it was a wrench to leave and come to somewhere new. I don't know Athens at all, and from what I've seen it looks big and busy, and I'll probably spend my whole time getting lost.'

Nikos caught the wistful note in her voice, and for the first time he appreciated just how hard it must have been for her to leave the island she loved. 'I will do my best to help you settle here,' he murmured. 'I haven't arranged a honeymoon, but I've taken some time off work so that I can show you around the city.' He paused, aware that for the first time in his life he felt awkward about how to treat a woman. Kitty was not any woman, she was his wife, and in a few months she would be the mother of his child. 'I was thinking about what you said last night,' he said quietly. 'And for the baby's sake I think you are right to suggest that we should get to know each other better, and to become…friends.'

Friends! Kitty gave a little start of shock. If she was honest she could not imagine being friends with Nikos. He was too remote, too forbidding, and way too sexy for her to believe they could establish a comfortable, friendly relationship. But wasn't this what she wanted? she reminded herself—an opportunity to learn more about the man behind the mask.

'As for your pregnancy feeling unreal, it may seem more real after we have seen the obstetrician,' Nikos continued. 'He has suggested an early scan to determine the date the baby is due.'

'That's not hard to work out. There is only one possible date that I could have conceived…' Once again hot colour flooded Kitty's cheeks and she dared not meet Nikos's gaze as she recalled the passion they had shared in the cave on the night of the royal ball. He could have no idea why she had refused to consummate their marriage last night, and no comprehension of her shyness in front of him or her insecurities about her body. But if he felt impatient he hid it well, and the unexpected warmth of his smile stole her breath.

'So what would you like to do today? I could show you the best places to shop in Athens. Ermou Street has some excellent boutiques.'

'If we are going to get to know each other better, then the first thing you should understand is that I hate shopping,' Kitty said firmly. 'But I would like to explore Athens. Have you always lived in the city?'

'Yes.' His smile faded. 'But the streets where I grew up are not on the tourist trail, and I'm sure you don't want a tour of the slums.'

Was he ashamed of his background? Kitty wondered. 'You aren't responsible for the circumstances of your birth,' she murmured. 'And you must be proud of all you have achieved. You are one of Greece's most successful businessmen.'

Nikos shrugged, but her words stayed in his mind. His success was phenomenal, but he had never stopped to consider his achievements. He had always been focused on the next deal, planning his next move up the corporate ladder. But he supposed he was proud—the boy from the gutter who had clawed his way to the top. He had never had anyone to share his success with before, but Kitty made him feel good about himself, and he realised suddenly that his new wife might appear quiet and shy, but she was deeply perceptive.

He relaxed back in his seat and smiled at her again, noting how the sun made her hair gleam like raw silk. 'If it's not to be shopping, where would you like to go?'

'The Parthenon, the Temple of Zeus, the

National Gardens.' Kitty listed the famous landmarks. 'You are a native Athenian, so I guess you know those places well.'

'I certainly do, *agape*.' He had never thought of himself as a native Athenian; he had always felt rootless and incomplete because he had no knowledge of who had fathered him. But it came to Nikos then that he was proud of his city and he wanted to show it to Kitty, and one day to their child who would be born here. 'Let's play tourists, then,' he said as he stood and held out his hand to her. 'I understand that you miss Aristo, but I will make you fall in love with Athens.'

Would Nikos also make her fall in love with him? Kitty brooded three days later as they walked around the National Archaeological Museum. He had been an enthusiastic guide showing her around the sights of the city, and during the days that they had spent together he had revealed some of the real Nikos Angelaki. She now knew that he kept his body in shape by playing squash and working out at the gym; that he liked sushi, and preferred to eat out with a few close friends rather than attend the lavish parties he was regularly invited to.

Stavros, his chauffer, and Sotiri, his butler, were clearly devoted to him, and Kitty was impressed that he engendered such loyalty from his staff. For such a wealthy and successful man, he appreciated the simple things in life—good food, good friends—and she had discovered a shared interest in contemporary films and authors, which had led to several long and interesting discussions when she had forgotten her shyness and chatted to him animatedly.

Away from the apartment at least, they seemed to be developing the friendship he had suggested, and even though she knew he was making an effort for the future, when they would be parents to their child, she clung to the nuggets of himself that he was willing to share. But back at the apartment the tension between them returned, brought about by the fierce sexual awareness that smouldered like a sleeping volcano between them and seemed in danger of erupting at any moment.

It was a situation she had brought on herself, Kitty admitted, thinking of the previous night when yet again she had been unable to sleep and had stared at the door connecting her room to his, wondering if she would ever have the courage to walk through it and end the deadlock. But she could not throw off her wariness. She was not afraid of the physical intimacy of sex, but she feared that if she gave herself totally to Nikos he would have a power over her that she was not ready to award him.

'Where to next?' His voice echoed faintly in the

vast, marble-floored museum and broke into her thoughts. 'Shall we carry on into the Sculptures Collection, or do you want to rest now? You look tired today, and for the baby's sake you don't want to overdo things.'

The only reason she was tired was because she had spent the night fantasising about him making love to her, Kitty acknowledged silently, blushing beneath Nikos's piercing gaze and praying he could not read her mind as he seemed able to do.

'I'd like to carry on,' she told him. 'Isn't it incredible to think that some of these pieces date back to the seventh century BC? We have a few ancient sculptures from the time of the Roman and Byzantine Empires in Aristo's museum, but the collection here in Greece is the most important in the world, and I can't tell you how thrilled I am to see it.'

'I'm glad you find something in Athens thrilling, *agape,*' Nikos taunted softly, feeling a mixture of amusement and impatience when Kitty blushed again. She was staring at him with her big, wary eyes; reminding him of a nervous deer poised to dash away should he venture too near.

At first, when she had refused to sleep with him, he had thought she was playing some sort of game. He had met women who used sex as a weapon and had no compunction about withholding it as a form of blackmail to get what they wanted, and he had cynically assumed that Kitty was no different. But he had learned these past few days that his wife *was* different. He had never met anyone like her before, but he was growing more and more convinced that her sweet, shy nature was not an act.

'If you are bored, we could go—and I'll come back another time,' she said anxiously.

'I'm not at all bored, *agape.* Your knowledge of your subject is quite astounding and you make a far more fascinating guide than the guidebook.' He was surprised to realise that he was speaking the truth. He enjoyed talking to Kitty and hearing about her work as a researcher at Aristo's Museum of History. She was fiercely intelligent and her passion for her work made her interesting.

He did not often have meaningful conversations with women, Nikos owned. His ex-lovers had invariably been models or socialites who talked predominantly about themselves or the latest gossip in the tabloids, and he had allowed them to witter on, and made suitable responses, during the necessary few dinner dates before he took them to bed.

With Kitty he could not give in to the urgent clamouring of his body and sweep her off to bed. He did not understand why she was holding back. He knew that she wanted him, and had had as little sleep as him for the past few nights, but he was not going to jump on her like some callow youth at the mercy of his hormones. He was determined to wait until she gave some indication that she had resolved the issues that clearly bothered her— and so he'd had no choice but to talk to her, and to his amazement he had discovered that he liked her as a person and would value her friendship.

'Actually, there's something in the next room that I want to show you,' she told him as they walked past the exhibits. 'This little figurine was sculpted round about five hundred and forty BC, and she was found about twenty years ago on Aristo—in the little fishing village, Varna. I remember you said that your mother's family came from there, and I thought you would be interested to see a little piece of your heritage.'

'My heritage?' Nikos frowned. 'I never knew my family in Varna. My grandparents cut off all contact with my mother when she fell pregnant with me and I don't suppose they even knew of my existence.'

'But even so, you have roots on Aristo,' Kitty insisted. 'I was thinking that it might be nice to trace your family tree. I can trace my ancestors back for generations, but one day our child will want to know about your side of the family.'

'You won't get far tracing my father. My mother took his identity with her to her grave,' Nikos said harshly.

'That must be strange,' Kitty said softly. 'I imagine you feel as though a part of you is missing. But to my mind that is even more reason to research your mother's side—so that we can give our child as complete a history as possible.'

She wandered off to look at the next exhibit, leaving Nikos staring after her. She was almost too perceptive, he brooded. Not knowing the identity of his father had always haunted him and Kitty had touched a nerve when she had guessed that he felt a part of him was missing. His child would make him feel whole, but he was unnerved by the realisation that Kitty probably guessed how much his baby meant to him.

The paparazzi were waiting for them when they walked out of the museum—a group of four or five sitting astride motor-scooters, who started snapping photographs despite Nikos's angry demand to stop.

'Someone must have recognised the car and tipped them off,' Stavros growled after he had opened the rear door for them to scramble inside, and then leapt into the driver's seat, pulling away from the kerb with a squeal of tyres.

'Then it's time to change the car,' Nikos replied tersely as he glanced out of the back window at the press-pack following close behind. He was used to a certain amount of media attention, but his marriage to a princess had been headline news around the world. Pictures showing him and Kitty together were selling for big money, and the photographers were growing increasingly aggressive as they fought for the shot that could make them a fortune. 'See if you can lose them, Stavros.'

'Aren't we going back to the apartment now?' Kitty queried, glancing at Nikos's shuttered expression.

'I'm afraid you are not going to like where we are going next,' he replied dryly, aware that the camaraderie between them was about to be blown to pieces. 'But the matter of your wardrobe has to be addressed, *agape,* and we are going shopping.'

Stavros was a skilled driver who seemed to know every back street in Athens. Eventually he lost the bikers and drew up in Kolonaki—an affluent district of the city famed for its designer boutiques. For the next couple of hours Kitty trailed around the shops while Nikos selected armfuls of outfits that she could tell from the bright colours and overtly sexy styles were not going to suit her.

'Try them on,' he bade her, the steely glint in his eyes warning her that arguing would be useless. The head saleswoman was clearly overawed by him and whisked them off to a private room so that Kitty could change in comfort. But when she stepped out from behind the curtain in a tight-fitting dress that left nothing to the imagination, she halted abruptly at the sight of Nikos sitting comfortably on the sofa, waiting for her.

'What are you doing?' she muttered beneath her breath, supremely conscious of the saleswoman nearby, and the fact that her breasts were in danger of spilling out of the dress. She had enjoyed his company at the museum, but shopping was a torture he had instigated, and she glared at him crossly.

'Giving my advice on what suits you,' he replied blandly. 'And having seen the clothes you brought from Aristo, believe me, you need help.' He trailed a deliberate path over her shapely figure, his dark eyes scorching her, and to Kitty's horror she felt her nipples harden.

'Very nice.' Nikos felt a shaft of desire surge through him as he pictured unlacing the ribbons that held the front of the dress together and releasing her magnificent breasts. He shifted slightly in his chair. 'We'll definitely take this one,' he told the saleswoman, his eyes still focused intently on Kitty as sexual tension crackled between them. She could feel her face grow hot, and her blush deepened when he gave her a mocking smile. 'Go and try on the next one,' he ordered. 'I haven't got all day.'

By the time they left the boutique, followed by three of the shop staff laden with bags, Kitty was flustered and furious. 'I hope you enjoyed humiliating me,' she muttered as they fought a path through the crowd who had gathered to see one of Greece's richest tycoons, and his royal bride.

'How did I humiliate you?' Nikos demanded impatiently.

'By making me try on all those things and parade around in front of you as if you owned me.' Kitty had felt excruciatingly self-conscious and convinced that he must have been comparing her voluptuous curves with his numerous skinny, blonde ex-lovers. 'None of the outfits you insisted on buying suited me, and it was a waste of money. They'll just sit at the back of the wardrobe because I'll never wear them.'

'Oh, but you will, *agape*.' He put a protective arm around her shoulder as someone in the crowd jostled her. Startled, Kitty glanced up and her eyes clashed with his mocking gaze. 'In fact you'll wear the red silk evening dress tonight. We've been invited to a party in aid of one of the charities I support, and all eyes will be on my wife.'

Kitty's horrified protest died on her lips when they emerged from the shop and were half blinded by the flash of a dozen cameras. The paparazzi had caught up with them. But fortunately Stavros was there and used his massive frame to shoulder a path to the car where he wrenched open the door so that Nikos could bundle Kitty inside.

'Why are they so interested?' Kitty cried as the car accelerated away and she watched the photographers weaving dangerously in and out of the traffic on their motor-scooters, in hot pursuit. 'It's not as if I've done anything to warrant such attention. I haven't done something wonderful for charity, or saved a life. I'm just drab, boring Kitty Karedes, who happens by an accident of birth to be a princess.'

'You are Kitty Angelaki now,' Nikos reminded her, 'and you are neither drab nor boring. But I agree that people seem to be increasingly celebrity obsessed.'

'The people on Aristo aren't,' Kitty muttered. 'Nothing like this ever happened to me there. I even used to ride around the island on my bike and the most attention anyone ever paid me was a smile or a wave.' She leaned her head back against the leather seat and placed her hand protectively on her stomach, more shaken than she cared to admit by the overwhelming media fascination with her. She felt desperately homesick for the peace and tranquillity of the palace, and the freedom that she had taken for granted on Aristo. Of course she'd had her royal duties to perform, but attending the opening of a new wing of the hospital had attracted only mild interest from the Aristan press and she wasn't used to being in the constant glare of the media spotlight.

She wished she could go home, back to where she felt safe. But home was now Nikos's elegant but characterless apartment that felt more like a five-star hotel than a comfortable bolt hole, and her misery was compounded by the news that tonight Nikos was taking her to a party where she would meet many of his sophisticated friends.

Sotiri greeted them when they walked into the apartment. 'Some boxes have arrived from Aristo for you, Miss Kitty,' he said, throwing open the door to the living room where four huge trunks were stacked.

'My books…' Kitty forgot the horrors of the shopping trip as she tore open one of the boxes and smiled at the sight of the dozens of books packed inside.

'*Theos*! Are *all* these crates full of books?' Nikos picked up a battered hardback. 'Where are you going to put them all? The apartment is spacious, but it's not big enough to house an entire library.'

'They're the books that I use for my research work, and I need them here,' Kitty said stubbornly.

'Well, there's no room for them in my study. I'll ask Sotiri to move the boxes into one of the spare bedrooms, and I suppose we can turn it into an office for you if you intend to carry on working—although

I doubt you'll have much free time, and of course financially there is no need for you to work.'

'I definitely want to carry on writing my book about the early history of the Adamas Islands, and I'd like to continue with my advisory work for Aristo's museum, certainly until the baby is born,' Kitty said slowly. 'If you are at your office all day, what else will I do?'

'I assumed you would want to get involved in charity work. A friend of mine, Melina Demakis, is a well-known social hostess in Athens who organises lunches and other fund-raising activities for a number of charities. I'll ask her to contact you.'

Kitty's heart sank at the prospect of filling her days lunching with wealthy and no doubt well-meaning doyennes of worthy organisations, and 'doing her bit' for charity. There had to be something more worthwhile she could do with her life, she thought heavily. 'I was thinking perhaps that I could volunteer to help out at the local hospital—visiting patients and maybe working a few hours in the coffee shop like I used to do at the hospital on Aristo.'

'You mean where you were once subjected to a vicious attack by a mentally ill patient? Sebastian told me that your father forbid you to go back there after the incident,' Nikos said in a scathing tone that showed what he thought of her idea.

'It wasn't a vicious attack. The patient lashed out and caught my cheek, but he didn't know what he was doing, poor man. My father was always rather overprotective,' Kitty added ruefully.

'As I am,' Nikos replied. 'How could you possibly work at a hospital with the paparazzi tailing your every move as they did today? You would be a hindrance rather than a help.'

'The paparazzi wouldn't know my whereabouts if I didn't draw attention to myself by turning up in a limousine, with a bodyguard at my side.'

'Well, you are certainly not stepping foot outside this apartment without Stavros,' Nikos said tersely. 'You are pregnant, Kitty, and I won't allow you to put yourself and our child in danger.'

'I have no intention of putting me or the baby in any sort of danger. But what do you mean by "won't allow"?' Kitty saw red as the empathy she had felt with him at the museum evaporated. 'Since when did you have authority over me?' she demanded furiously.

'Since you became my wife—and, more importantly, since you conceived my baby,' he replied in a tone that brooked no further argument. He glanced at his watch and strolled down the hall. 'I have an hour's work to do in my study. I suggest you start preparing for the party. From past experience I know how long it takes women to get ready.'

That final reference to his previous women—
with emphasis on the plural—was the final
straw, and Kitty was seriously tempted to fling
the porcelain figurine of Aphrodite that stood
on the hall dresser at his head. But Nikos had
disappeared into his study, and after a few
minutes she trailed down the hall and through
the master bedroom to her dressing room,
carried on into the en suite and ran herself a
bath, hoping that a long soak in fragrant bubbles
would relieve her growing tension at the
prospect of socialising with a hoard of people
she had never met before.

An hour later she stood in front of the mirror and
studied her reflection with dismay. The floor-length
evening gown made from rich ruby-red satin had a
strapless, tight-fitting bodice, and an even tighter
fitting skirt that clung to her hips and bottom and
flared out from mid-thigh, with a side split that at
least enabled her to walk. It was the most daringly
sexy dress she had ever seen, let alone possessed—
and it made her look like a tart, she decided grimly
as she turned sideways to the mirror and sucked in
her stomach. Any woman who wore this dress
would attract attention. But that was the last thing
she wanted to do at tonight's party.

If she had realised how much of her body was
displayed by the plunging neckline she would
have sneaked it back on the rail in the shop, Kitty

thought fiercely as she tugged the zip down and stepped out of the dress.

The black evening dress she'd brought from Aristo was not unattractive, and at least it didn't make her look as if she walked the streets for a living. Even better, it would draw no attention at all, and with luck she could slink into a corner and remain there for the evening.

She swept her hair up into a knot on top of her head, exchanged the four-inch stilettos that matched the red dress for black two-inch kitten heels, and walked through the connecting door just as Nikos emerged from his bathroom.

He was devastating in a black tuxedo and a white silk shirt, his bow tie as yet unfastened and hanging open at his throat. He looked every inch the urbane, sophisticated, billionaire tycoon, with a raw sex appeal that would make every woman at the party go weak at the knees. Kitty felt a fierce tug of sexual awareness that made her heart race and her breath catch in her throat. But from the expression on his face, he was clearly not impressed by her appearance, and his brows lowered in a slashing frown as he walked towards her.

'Not quite what I had in mind, *agape*,' he drawled as his eyes slid down from her severe hairstyle to her prim, plain dress. 'I thought we had decided that you would wear the red dress?'

'No, you decided I would wear the red dress,'

Kitty snapped. 'But I refuse to go out looking like a hooker you've picked up from some bar.'

'You prefer to go out looking as though you are on your way to a funeral?' His brows rose, and Kitty itched to wipe the arrogant expression from his face. 'You have five minutes to change,' he said in a dangerously soft voice. 'You are my wife, Kitty, and I expect you to dress accordingly, not wear something that makes you resemble a maiden aunt.'

Kitty's temper had been simmering since their argument about her working at the hospital, and it ignited at his heavy-handedness.

'I feel more comfortable wearing clothes of my choice,' she began, and then emitted a startled cry when his hands shot out and wrenched the front of her dress open so that the buttons running from neck to waist pinged in all directions.

'What do you think you're doing? *How dare you*?' She was breathing hard, her chest heaving so that Nikos's attention was drawn to her breasts, which were barely contained in a semi-transparent black bra.

'I dare, Kitty *mou*,' he drawled, his voice no longer sharp with annoyance but thick with sexual desire that caused an answering shiver of awareness to run down her spine, 'because you are my wife.' With deft fingers he tugged the pins from her hair so that it fell down her back in a river of silk. 'You now have two minutes to exchange dresses, or risk me removing what is left of this one,' he warned her silkily. 'And if I strip you completely I think it's a safe bet that we won't be going anywhere but my bed tonight.'

The determined gleam in his eyes told Kitty that he meant it too. A dignified retreat seemed her only option, and, head held high, she swung round and marched into her room, venting her temper by slamming the connecting door, and grinding her teeth when she heard his mocking laughter through the thin walls.

She hated him, she told her reflection, tears of mortification stinging her eyes as she stepped out of her ruined dress and squeezed herself into the red ball-gown. He was the most arrogant, overbearing man she had ever met—and it was a bitter irony that he was the only man who had ever made her ache with desire.

Because she wanted him, she acknowledged with reluctant honesty. She had wanted him that night in the cave, and she wanted him now. It was not fear of the physical act of making love with him that had made her sleep in another room, but the fear of giving herself to him, body and soul, and receiving nothing in return.

She could very easily fall in love with him, she thought bleakly as she ran a brush through her hair so that it fell around her shoulders like a curtain of silk. But she would be a fool to lose her heart to him, because his was carved from ice, and he had made it clear that it would never melt.

The connecting door swung open, and for a second her eyes clashed with Nikos's unfathomable gaze reflected in the mirror. Quickly she lowered her lashes, praying he had not guessed her thoughts, but her heart was hammering when he came to stand behind her.

'I knew the dress would suit you. You look stunning.'

Kitty had spent her whole adult life longing to be told she looked attractive, but Nikos's coolly delivered compliment left her feeling strangely deflated. He was just being polite, she decided. He was probably thinking that her bottom looked huge, and regretting on insisting that she should wear the dress.

'It's really not my style,' she muttered, her cheeks burning when his eyes slid over her and lingered on her voluptuous breasts that were thrusting provocatively above the tight-fitting bodice. 'I want to wear something else, Nikos—another of the dresses we bought today.' Preferably one that was less eye-catching.

'Don't be ridiculous.' He could not hide the impatience in his voice. 'And don't keep looking down at the floor.' He swung her round and caught her chin between his fingers, tilting her face to his. 'A dress like this needs to be worn with confidence.' From his jacket he extracted a narrow velvet box, which he opened to reveal an exquisite ruby and diamond pendant suspended on a gold chain. He smiled when Kitty gave an audible gasp. 'This matches the dress perfectly,' he murmured as he fastened it around her neck.

His hands were warm against her skin, but Kitty shivered as he swung her back round to face the mirror. Once again her eyes locked with his and she felt the familiar, prickling tension between them. The pulse at the base of her throat was plainly visible, beating erratically beneath her skin, and she caught her breath when he lowered his head and brushed his mouth along her collarbone.

'Time to go, Kitty *mou*.' His voice was deep and husky, and sent another shiver of acute awareness down her spine. 'Have pity on me tonight,' he murmured, his mouth curving into a self-derisive smile as he stepped away from her. 'Every time I look at you I will be imagining you wearing nothing but the necklace.'

She swallowed hard at the feral hunger in his eyes. 'You shouldn't say things like that.'

He shrugged. 'Why not, when it's the truth? And before much longer the image in my head will be reality. My patience is wearing thin, *agape*,' he warned her silkily, and turned and walked out of the room, leaving Kitty staring after him, her heart thumping.

CHAPTER TEN

THE charity gala was being held at an exclusive five-star hotel in the heart of Athens. As the car drew up outside the front steps and Kitty glanced out of the window at the blinding flashbulbs from the paparazzi's cameras she felt the familiar sick dread in the pit of her stomach. Some of her tension must have shown on her face because Nikos frowned as he leaned towards her.

'Relax, *agape*. You look as though you are about to be thrown to the lions rather than attend a party where you are the star guest.'

'I'd rather be thrown into a lions' den,' Kitty muttered.

'You're not still worried about your dress, are you?' Now there was an edge of impatience in Nikos's voice. 'I told you, you look stunning, and all eyes will be on you.'

'I don't *want* everyone to notice me. I've

always been hopeless at socialising,' Kitty admitted miserably.

'But you must have regularly attended parties and functions at the palace.'

'Yes, but I never enjoyed it. Liss was always the party girl, and she has the looks and confidence to walk into a room full of strangers. I just get tongue-tied and never know what to say to people. I'm afraid you're going to find me a big disappointment, Nikos,' she finished gloomily.

'I did not realise you found socialising such an ordeal,' he murmured, taken aback by her revelation. 'But I assure you I will not find you a disappointment, Kitty. And I will be by your side constantly to introduce you to people. Have you ever thought that they might be nervous about meeting you?' he queried.

'Why would anyone feel nervous about meeting me?' Kitty demanded, startled.

'Because you are a princess. I think a lot of people could feel overawed by your royal status, not to mention the fact that you are intelligent and highly educated. Think about it,' Nikos murmured as Stavros opened the car door and he stepped out, turning back to assist Kitty in alighting from the car.

She was so shocked by the idea that people might be unnerved by meeting her that she barely noticed the press pack jostling around them, and she gave a shocked gasp when Nikos put his arm around her waist and dipped his head to kiss her full on the mouth. His lips were warm and firm and she responded to him without conscious thought, her eyes wide with confusion when he broke the kiss after a disappointingly short time.

'Why did you do that?' she mumbled as he drew her hand through his arm and escorted her up the steps and into the hotel.

'We are newly-weds, Kitty *mou*,' he reminded her, his eyes gleaming with amusement and something else that made her stomach dip. 'I thought it was about time we gave the paparazzi something to photograph.'

The moment they walked into the ballroom, they were the centre of attention—Athens's most famous billionaire shipping magnate and his princess bride. Glancing around at the female guests in their couture gowns and spectacular jewellery, Kitty reluctantly had to admit that she would have stuck out like a sore thumb in her drab black dress. But there was no chance of her slinking into a quiet corner in the daring red gown, and Nikos stayed true to his word and did not leave her side. Instead he moved seamlessly from one group of guests to the next, introducing Kitty, and initiating conversation on topics he knew she was interested in so that she had something to say.

To her utter amazement she realised that Nikos

had been right and that many of the people she met were not actually stiff and unfriendly as she had thought, but that they felt awkward in the presence of royalty and did not know quite how to treat her. Anxious to put them at their ease, she forgot her shyness and chatted to them, and to her surprise she discovered halfway through the evening that she was enjoying herself.

This really wasn't so bad, she mused later as she strolled over to the bar and asked the waiter for a fruit juice. Seeing that her confidence had soared, Nikos had left her for a few minutes to go and talk to one of his business associates, but Kitty was not alone for long.

'Princess Katarina? My name is Darius Christakis. I'm a lecturer at the university of Athens.'

She had noticed the man looking at her several times during the evening, and now, as he held out his hand to her, Kitty smiled and returned his greeting.

'Mr Christakis.'

He was very good-looking, she mused, and he was attracting interested glances from several women around the room. But he appeared to only have eyes for her, and she was startled when faint colour flared in his face.

'Darius, please.'

'And I'm Kitty,' she murmured, wanting to put

him at his ease. 'The whole royal title thing is a bit of a mouthful, don't you think?'

'Actually, I think you are amazing.' The young man's flush deepened. 'I studied your paper on The Crusades during the twelfth century and the impact on Greece and the surrounding Mediterranean islands, and to be honest it was one of the most fascinating pieces I've ever read.' Darius grinned sheepishly. 'I must admit I imagined you to look like a learned scholar with glasses and a tweed skirt, but instead I find that you are gorgeous—if you don't mind my saying so,' he added, raking a hand distractedly through his hair.

'I don't mind,' Kitty said with a laugh, her self-confidence boosted by his description of her. If only he knew that a few weeks ago she *had* been a frumpy scholar, more interested in her books than her looks, but as she saw the undisguised admiration in Darius's eyes she felt a spurt of gratitude to Nikos who had transformed her from drab to, apparently, gorgeous.

'I was wondering if you would consider being a guest speaker at the university?' Darius continued. 'Your work at the museum on Aristo is well known and my students would really enjoy meeting you.'

Kitty's heart lurched at the idea of public speaking. But it would be on her specialist subject, and she would enjoy visiting Athens's university. On a sudden rush of confidence she nodded to Darius. 'I'd love to.'

'Great.' He beamed at her. 'Maybe we could get together soon to discuss your visit?'

'I'm afraid my wife will need to consult her diary before she makes any commitments.' Nikos materialised at Kitty's side, his dark brows drawn into a frown as he slid his arm possessively around her waist and clamped her so hard against him that she could barely breathe.

'Nikos, this is Darius Christakis…' Kitty began, breaking off at the look of open hostility in Nikos' eyes as he glared at the younger man.

'I see that your companions are waiting for you, Mr Christakis,' he said in a dangerously soft tone. 'You'd better go back to them.'

'Right.' The younger man backed away, gave Kitty a brief, nervous smile and shot off across the room.

'That was incredibly rude of you.' She rounded on Nikos the moment the other man was out of earshot. 'He only wanted to talk about a paper I'd written.'

'He wanted to dive into the front of your dress, *agape*,' Nikos drawled sardonically, his eyes glinting as he stared at Kitty's angry face. 'I've noticed the way he's been looking at you all night.'

'Nonsense…' She paused, blushing when she

recalled how Darius had called her gorgeous. 'Anyway, it was you who insisted I should wear this dress.'

'A decision I am now regretting,' Nikos murmured as he led her onto the dance floor and drew her into his arms. 'You are attracting too much male attention, and I have discovered that I am very possessive. In future you can wear something beige and baggy to hide your delectable body from everyone but me.'

He was teasing her, surely, Kitty thought, her eyes widening when she realised that the expression in his dark gaze was deadly serious. 'Are you...*jealous*, Nikos?' She blushed scarlet as the words left her lips, certain that he would deny it. Instead his eyes narrowed and he tightened his arms around her so that her pelvis came into direct contact with the shockingly hard ridge of his arousal.

'It is not an emotion I am familiar with, Kitty *mou*,' he murmured dulcetly, 'but if you so much as look at another man for the hour or so remaining until we can leave, I will demonstrate in front of everyone here just how possessive I am of my wife—and how very impatient I am to make love to her.'

'Nikos!' Kitty could not hold back her shocked cry, or restrain the quiver of white-hot sexual awareness that ripped through her. This had been building for the past few days, she acknowledged numbly as she stared at him and saw the sensual gleam beneath his heavy lids. The drumbeat of desire that she had tried so hard to ignore was now thudding deep inside her, sending her blood coursing through her veins. They were moving in time with the music, their bodies locked together so that she could feel every muscle and sinew of his hard thighs pressed against her softer flesh.

'You take my breath away tonight—my lady in red,' he murmured, his voice so low and husky in her ear that it seemed to reverberate right through her. She could feel the faint abrasion of his cheek against her face and knew that if she turned her head a fraction their mouths would meet. Her heartbeat quickened when he slid his hand into her hair, and when he exerted gentle pressure she lifted her face to him and felt his breath warm her skin before his lips claimed hers in a deep, slow kiss—a sensual tasting that she was powerless to resist.

The other guests on the dance floor faded away and the music of the band seemed distant. Nothing existed but Nikos: the strength of his arms holding her close against his chest, and the languorous drift of his mouth moving over hers in a drugging kiss that seemed to last a lifetime. Kitty responded to him helplessly, her wariness and insecurities forgotten as the fire inside her flamed into urgent life, and she murmured her protest when at last he lifted his head.

'Time to go home,' he growled as he whisked her off the dance floor and headed determinedly in the direction of their host.

It was on the tip of Kitty's tongue to tell him that it would be impolite to leave halfway through the party, but her brain seemed to have stopped functioning, and her body was burning up. In the car on the way back across town she tried to remind herself of the reasons why she had held out against making love with Nikos—but he no longer seemed the remote stranger he had been on their wedding day. He had been a kind and charming companion for the past few days when he had shown her around Athens, and she had found herself falling under his spell. As for her worries that he could not really be attracted to her when he had previously dated beautiful blonde models—he had only had eyes for her tonight, and his self-confessed jealousy when she had chatted to the university lecturer had made her feel like a desirable woman.

She was a mass of confused emotions when the lift whisked them up to the apartment and she dared not look at Nikos even though she knew he was staring at her with his dark, brooding gaze. The tension between them was tangible, and she gasped when the lift doors opened and he suddenly scooped her into his arms as if she weighed nothing.

'What are you doing?' She clutched his shoulders and looked into his face, her heart pounding when she saw the determined glint in his eyes.

'What I wanted to do when we first arrived here on our wedding day,' he told her as he strode down the hall and into the master bedroom, where the blinds were drawn and the room was bathed in a soft apricot glow from the bedside lamps. 'And what we both want now,' he added as he set her on her feet. 'Your body has been sending out signals all night, *agape*.' And for the past few days if she had but known it, Nikos brooded, recalling every shy smile she had given him, the way she often moistened her lips with the tip of her pink tongue in an unconscious invitation and the way she stared at him with her big brown eyes when she thought he wouldn't notice. For the past few nights he had lain awake aching with frustration, fighting the temptation to walk through the connecting door and snatch her into his arms.

'I want you to be my wife in every sense, Kitty,' he said deeply, running his finger lightly down her cheek and noting how her pupils had dilated so that her eyes seemed too big for her delicate face. 'I want to recapture the passion we once shared, and I dare you to deny that you want that too.

'Your body has already given you away, *agape*,' he growled when she made no reply. Following his gaze, she looked down and saw the stiff peaks of her nipples straining against her silk dress, and she caught her breath when he cupped her breasts and caressed them, brushing his fingers across their swollen crests so that sensation pierced her. Her dress was an intolerable barrier. She was desperate to feel his hands on her naked flesh, and suddenly nothing else mattered except that he should appease the desire that was flooding through her in an unstoppable torrent.

But she did not know what to say—how to tell him that she was ready to be his wife. Actions seemed easier than words. Her heart was thudding painfully beneath her ribs as, eyes locked with his, she reached behind her and drew the zip of her dress down from her neck to her waist. For a second he did not react, and tension screamed between them before he brought his mouth down on hers in a kiss of utter possession that told her clearer than any words that she had made her decision and there would be no going back.

The bodice of Kitty's dress was boned, meaning that she hadn't needed to wear a bra. As Nikos drew the red silk down lower and lower her breasts emerged like plump peaches and spilled into his hands. Instantly he felt his body stir, and for a second he was tempted to rip the dress from her body, throw her down on the bed and take her hard and fast. But with formidable will power he curbed his impatience. He could sense her lingering uncertainty, and he knew he must take it slow and arouse her fully until she ached as he ached with hot sexual frustration that clamoured for release.

He pushed her dress down over her hips and tugged it down her thighs until it slithered to the floor. Through the lacy panel of her knickers he could see the dark shadow of silky hair that shielded her femininity, and he heard her swift indrawn breath when he hooked his fingers into the waistband and stripped her completely.

When he had made love to her that first and only time in the cave she had been half hidden in shadow. But now her body was exposed in all its voluptuous glory and he feasted his eyes on her, gently moving her hands down when she tried to cover her breasts. 'Why do you want to hide yourself from me?' he queried softly. 'You are beautiful, Kitty, and I have never wanted any woman the way I want you.'

Kitty trembled at his words, and watched, wide eyed, as he deftly removed his own clothes, dropping his shirt and trousers carelessly to the floor to reveal his hard, muscular chest and thighs. His silk boxers could not disguise the jutting length of his erection, and she snatched a sharp little breath when he stepped out of them and stood before her, his awesome arousal sending a flicker of trepidation through her.

But then he caught her to him and crushed her

soft, pliant body against the hardness of his as he slanted his mouth over hers and kissed her until she could think of nothing but him and her desperate need for him to touch her between her legs and soothe the throbbing ache that began low in her stomach. His tongue delved between her lips, taking the kiss to a deeper level, and she responded mindlessly, matching his fierce passion until he groaned and lifted her onto the bed, coming down beside her with one thigh across her hip to anchor her to the sheets.

'You have magnificent breasts, Kitty *mou*.' There was no hint of teasing in his low tone, just raw, feral need that sent an answering shaft of desire through her and made her arch her back when he traced his mouth down from her lips to the deep valley of her cleavage. The flick of his tongue across one dusky, swollen nipple and then its twin was so exquisite that she cried out and dug her fingers into his thick black hair to hold him to her breasts. His soft laughter feathered her skin, and when he took each stiff crest in turn into his mouth and sucked hard she twisted her hips restlessly and felt damp heat flood between her legs.

'Nikos…' The last shadows in her mind were blown away when he slid his hand over her stomach to her thighs and rested there, tantalisingly close to where she longed for him to touch her. She held her breath when he gently parted her, and when he slid his finger into her and caressed her with rhythmic strokes she spread her legs a little wider so that he could continue his erotic foreplay.

She could feel the solid length of his erection pushing against her thigh, and a tremor of shock ran through her when he took her hand and placed it on his arousal. He was so hard and powerful, and any second now she was going to have to take him inside her. She had done so once before, she reminded herself as panic fluttered in her stomach. But then he moved over her, slid his hand beneath her bottom to lift her slightly, and there was no time for doubt because he eased forwards and entered her with one sure thrust that made her gasp as he filled her.

For a moment he stilled and stared down at her, his dark eyes burning into hers. Then he began to move; firm, steady strokes as he drove into her, setting a pagan rhythm that echoed the drumbeat of her heart and sent her blood thundering through her veins. She could feel the tension inside her spiral with each exquisite thrust, and now he moved faster, harder, taking them inexorably towards the edge. Kitty felt as though she was losing her grip on reality, lost to sensation and the pleasure that was building and building. She clung to his shoulders and anchored there while the storm raged. Little ripples were starting deep inside her and radiating out as her climax hovered tantalisingly close. Desperation made her sob his name, and she pleaded with him to never, ever stop. And suddenly she was there, suspended for timeless seconds while he withdrew almost fully, and then with his next powerful thrust the dam broke and she was racked by spasm after spasm of intense sensation that dragged a sharp, animal cry from her throat.

Still he continued to move, each thrust more forceful and urgent than the last. But the feel of her vaginal muscles tightening around him, squeezing him, shattered his formidable control, and with a harsh groan Nikos spilled his seed inside her, his big body shuddering with the power of his release and his chest heaving as he dragged oxygen into his lungs.

In the aftermath Kitty lay still, and stared dazedly at the ceiling. His head lay on her breasts and she crossed her arms around his back, swamped by the same feeling she'd had in the cave when she had lost her virginity to him: that their souls were inextricably linked. It was an illusion of course, she told herself firmly, brought about by the intensity of the passion they had just shared. For Nikos it was simply good sex—a fact that he emphasised when he rolled off her and stretched his lean body out on the silk sheets, tucking his arms behind his head as if he were a sultan who had just enjoyed the services of his favourite concubine.

'You see, *agape*,' he murmured lazily. 'Our sexual compatibility is not in doubt.' He drew a ragged breath, waiting for his heartbeat to slow and wondering why he had felt so reluctant to withdraw from her. He would have liked to pillow his head on her breasts and simply lie with her. But the curious feeling of closeness that had swamped him in the aftermath of their lovemaking wasn't real, he assured himself. It was just good sex that he hadn't wanted to end. Fantastic sex; the best he'd had in a long time. Perhaps ever, his mind taunted him. It didn't mean anything. He had married Kitty because he wanted his child, and the fact that sex with her was dynamite was an added bonus that left his body satisfied and his heart untouched.

Kitty's skin had quickly cooled without the heat and welcome weight of Nikos's body pressing down on her, and she longed to curl up against him and lay her head on his chest. But now that he no longer filled her she sensed a distance between them far greater than the width of the bed. For her own self-protection it was vital she rebuilt her defences against him. She did not know what he expected now that he had made love to her. He seemed suddenly remote, lost in his thoughts, and she wanted to escape to the privacy of her own room, but when she sat up and swung her legs over the side of the bed he reached out and curled his arm around her waist.

'Where are you going?'

'I thought I would sleep in my room.'

His eyes narrowed on her flushed face and he sensed the tension that once more gripped her. 'It's too late to run away now, *agape*. You are mine, and from now on you will sleep with me. Besides,' he murmured as he drew her back down and moved over her, 'I intend to make love to you several times during the night and it would be most inconvenient if I had to trek backwards and forwards to fetch you.'

Beneath his teasing tone was a wealth of sensual promise that caused a tugging sensation low in Kitty's stomach. 'Several times?' she murmured faintly.

'Certainly, *agape*,' he assured her, 'starting now.'

Kitty watched their reflection in the wall of mirrors; Nikos's dark head bent to her breast, and she inhaled sharply when he painted moist circles around one areola with his tongue and then drew her nipple into his mouth. She ran her fingers through his hair, and then paused when she noticed for the first time the tattoo of a scorpion on his shoulder.

'What is this?' she asked, remembering how Vasilis had said that Nikos had once been part of the criminal underworld.

He followed her gaze to his reflection in the mirror, and his face hardened. 'A reminder of my past—it is the mark of the street gang I used to belong to when I was a youth. Stavros and Sotiri were members of the same gang, and we used to make money from illegal bare-knuckle boxing in back-street clubs.'

'Dear God!' She could not keep the shock from her voice. 'How old were you?'

He shrugged. 'Fifteen—but as I was bigger than most of my opponents, none of the sharks who organised the fights cared too much.'

'You mean you fought men, even though you were not much more than a boy?' Kitty felt sick and her horror must have shown in her eyes because Nikos grimaced.

'Many things in my past are not pretty, *agape*. I had a tough childhood—but our child will not have to fight to survive,' he vowed fiercely, placing a hand on her stomach as if to protect the tiny life she carried. 'I grew up knowing hunger and deprivation, and there were many times when my mother had no money to pay the rent and we were evicted onto the streets. But even though life was hard I never doubted her love for me. She worked herself quite literally to death to feed and care for me.'

The words were torn from his throat. Words he had never spoken to anyone before, and he wondered why he felt this urge to unburden the memories of his past to Kitty. Her brown eyes were gentle and velvet soft, and she made no comment, simply waited patiently for him to continue.

'My mother was terrified I would fall into a life of crime,' he admitted grimly, 'but when I was sixteen she was offered a job as housekeeper for Larissa Petridis, and I was allowed to live with her in the staff quarters of the Petridis mansion. Stamos Petridis had died some years before and had left Petridis Shipping to his only daughter. Larissa had never married and had no children of her own but she took an interest in me. She offered to pay to send me to college, and, although it hurt my pride, I accepted, knowing that if I gained a degree I could get a good job and support my mother as she had supported me.'

He rolled onto his back, his jaw rigid as the memories he had pushed away for so long returned to haunt him. 'My mother died of cancer before I graduated. *Theos*, she was only in her early thirties,' he grated, his voice cracking, 'but the hardships she had suffered during her life had taken their toll, and when she became ill she had no strength to fight the disease. For a while I was crazy with grief but Larissa persuaded me to make something of my life. She offered me a position within her company and I quickly demonstrated a flair for business—although there was some gossip that my rise to top management was because I was Larissa's lover.

'The rumours were unfounded,' he told Kitty. 'I looked upon Larissa as a surrogate mother, and she treated me like the son she had never had—although it amused her to allow the media to think there was something between us. Larissa was what you might call a character,' he added dryly.

'When she died suddenly I was as shocked as anyone when I learned that she had made me her sole beneficiary. I took charge of the company, and I've worked hard to make it successful.'

He broke off, his eyes dark and tortured, and Kitty's heart turned over. 'I'm sure Larissa would have been proud of you,' she said softly. She had heard the affection in his voice when he spoke of the woman who had befriended him—yet Larissa had died only a few short years after his mother and once again he had been left alone. No wonder he seemed so hard and ruthless. His father had abandoned him before he had been born, and he had lost the only two people he had loved. She wanted to weep for the lonely boy he had once been, and the man who had built an impenetrable wall around his heart. Acting on instinct, and uncaring that she might reveal too much of herself to him, she cupped his face in her hands and brought her mouth to his in a kiss that offered comfort and understanding and a tenderness that shook Nikos to his core.

Passion built swiftly between them and he moved over her and entered her, taking them both to the heights of pleasure. It was just good sex; he repeated the mantra in his head as he drove into her and felt his pleasure build and build until it was intolerable and he could hold back no longer. Sexual alchemy was a potent force that held them both in its thrall, but that was *all* it was, he assured himself as her soft cries shattered the last remnants of his control.

But afterwards, as he lay with his head on her breasts, he felt more relaxed than he could ever remember. And later, when he lay beside her and she curled up against him, he slept peacefully for the first time in years.

CHAPTER ELEVEN

SUNLIGHT slanting through the blinds roused Kitty from a deep sleep. She stretched, and rolled over, smiling at the sight of the cup of camomile tea that Nikos had placed on her bedside table. She was now into the second month of her pregnancy and often woke feeling nauseous. The herbal tea was the only thing that seemed to settle her stomach, and Nikos made it for her every morning, and would not allow her out of bed until she had drunk it.

She had seen a new side to him these past couple of weeks, she mused. He still seemed remote sometimes, and he worked long hours, driven, she guessed, by the demons of his impoverished childhood. But most nights he came home in time for them to eat dinner together, even though he often carried on working in his study for a few hours afterwards. She looked forward to their shared meals. Face it, Nikos coming home was the highlight of her day, she admitted wryly. She enjoyed their conversations about her work and his, or their lively discussions about events in the news. She was as passionate about politics as she was about history, and in Nikos she had found someone who was happy to challenge her views and state his own. He made her feel alive in a way no other man ever had—and when he swept her off to bed every night and made love to her with skilled passion, he gave her body more pleasure than she had believed was possible.

Since the night of the charity gala that had ended with them consummating their marriage they had attended numerous parties and social events, and she was slowly beginning to find it less nerve-racking when she walked into a room full of strangers. Unlike on Aristo where she had managed to avoid the limelight, people in Athens seemed fascinated by her royal status and wherever she went she was the focus of avid interest from Nikos's wide circle of friends and business associates.

But it was difficult not to attract attention when Nikos insisted on her wearing the glamorous gowns that now filled her wardrobe. The clothes she had brought from Aristo had mysteriously disappeared, and been replaced by elegant daywear, and exotic, overtly sexy cocktail dresses and ball-gowns that she would never have chosen for herself. Sometimes she wondered if he was trying to turn her into a woman more like the sophisticated models he had dated before he had married her, but her insecurities about her body were gradually fading and her self-confidence growing as she blossomed beneath his attention and his undisguised desire for her.

She could hear the sounds of the shower and knew that he would emerge from the en suite dressed in one of his designer suits that he wore for work. He would look as gorgeous as ever, but a glance in the mirror revealed that her hair looked like a bush and her face was a peculiar shade of green. The nausea was bad again this morning. Yesterday she had actually been sick, but fortunately not until after Nikos had gone.

She sat up slowly, praying the feeling would pass. She couldn't bear the idea of throwing up while he was around. It would be so undignified, she thought miserably, but her body cared nothing for dignity, and with a gasp she shot off the bed and raced through the connecting door to her dressing room and bathroom.

Nikos found her there five minutes later, and, ignoring her terse plea to go away and leave her alone, he remained with her while she lost the contents of her stomach, and then wiped her face with a damp cloth as if she were a helpless child.

'Are you feeling any better?' he asked quietly

when she sat on the edge of the bath, ashen-faced and utterly spent. For some reason the concern in his voice angered her. He wasn't asking because he cared about her; he was only worried about the baby. She caught sight of her reflection in the mirror, and tears stung her eyes when she saw her sallow skin and her hair hanging limp and lustreless on her shoulders. She looked disgusting, and she felt embarrassed about him seeing her at her most vulnerable and unattractive.

'I *hate* feeling like this,' she admitted miserably.

Nikos stiffened at her words. 'It is a natural side effect of pregnancy. The doctor said the sickness should lessen in a few more weeks.'

He made her sound as though she was making a huge fuss over something trivial, and Kitty glared at him. 'Well, he would say that, he's a man, and he's never had to go through this.' Any more than Nikos had. The unspoken words hung in the air. 'You have no idea how revolting I feel right now,' she told him tightly. 'It's okay for you. Your body isn't going to change out of all recognition and blow up like a balloon, and you don't have to worry that whatever you eat for dinner is likely to bounce back up before breakfast.'

'True,' he said in a clipped tone, his dark eyes focused intently on her as if he was determined to read her mind. 'But it will be worth it in the end—when the baby is here.'

'I suppose,' Kitty muttered. Now she was ashamed of her silly outburst, and for some reason she wanted to cry, but not in front of him. Hormones had a lot to answer for, she thought heavily. 'I'm fine now,' she assured him. 'Go to work, Nikos.'

He hesitated. 'If it was any other day I would cancel my engagements and stay home. But I have a series of important meetings scheduled.'

She was desperate for him to go so that she could shower and wash her hair, try and make herself look vaguely human. 'I don't need you here,' she told him edgily. 'The nausea is passing, and in a while I'll eat something.' When he still did not move she cast around her mind for something to convince him she was perfectly all right. 'I thought I might look into some charities that I could support. You said you have a friend who organises fund-raising events,' she prompted him.

'Yes, Melina Demakis. I'll find you her number. But I don't want you to take on too much. Your main priority should be caring for your health, and that of the baby.'

'I realise that, and I will take care of myself.' Kitty thought of the lonely hours she had spent in the apartment since he had returned to work. 'You're at your office all day, and I can't just sit around for the next seven months until the baby comes.'

He stared at her for a moment more and then

nodded. 'All right—come with me now and I'll give you Melina's contact details.'

Nikos's office was decorated in the same minimalist style as the rest of the apartment, pale walls and black furniture, a couple of modern prints in silver frames on the walls. The only personal item in the room was a small framed photograph on his desk.

'My mother,' he said when Kitty glanced curiously at the picture of a woman with dark hair and a gentle smile. 'That was taken when I was a child. I found it among her things after she died. It's the only photo I have of her,' he added, taking the picture from Kitty and staring down at it.

'She was very pretty,' she murmured, 'and she looks kind.'

'She was.'

Kitty was startled by the flare of pain in his eyes, but it was quickly hidden behind the sweep of his thick lashes. He set the photo down without further comment and flipped open the address book on his desk. 'Melina's details are here. I'm afraid I must go, I'm running late, and I may not be back for dinner. But Sotiri will cook for you, so make sure you eat—for the baby's sake.'

His concern for his child was indisputable, Kitty thought when he had gone. Naturally she wanted to do what was best for the baby, but sometimes Nikos made her feel more like an incubator than an expectant mother.

By late morning she was feeling more like her usual self, and when she had showered and dressed, and eaten a huge breakfast, the day stretched before her. She had phoned Melina Demakis and spoken at length about possible charities she might like to support, and had arranged to meet the older woman and several of her committee members the following week. It seemed that she was destined to spend her life attending fund-raising events, and because of her royal status she was likely to bring attention to the organisations she supported, but it seemed an empty existence, and she wished she could do something more worthwhile.

She flicked idly through the daily newspaper, pausing when a familiar name caught her attention. She had met Father Thomaso a few years ago when she had opened a hospice on Aristo that he had raised funds for. Now in his late sixties, the priest was at an age when he could have retired, but instead he was living in Athens and had set up a charity to help underprivileged young people.

In the article Father Thomaso spoke movingly of the problems facing the very poor, especially children and teenagers—many of whom were immigrants who had come to Athens for a better life and had ended up living in slums or rough on the streets. He had opened a youth centre to provide a place of safety for children and adolescents, and was asking for financial and practical support.

Deeply touched by the case stories she had read, Kitty picked up the phone, and when she set it down again twenty minutes later she had arranged to visit the Father and his youth centre to see what she could do to help.

Later that day Kitty stared worriedly out of the taxi window at the volume of traffic on the road. She had stayed at the youth centre for much longer than she had planned, and a glance at her watch told her that she was going to be seriously late to meet Stavros at the National Archaeological Museum.

Up until now her plan had worked well— although she didn't feel comfortable about tricking Stavros, or deceiving Nikos. She wasn't really deceiving him, she told herself. She had actually phoned his office to tell him she was going to visit the youth centre run by Father Thomaso, but his secretary had said he was in a meeting and had given instructions not to be disturbed unless there was an emergency.

She could have left a message, Kitty acknowledged. But it had seemed easier to keep her plans to herself. Nikos had forbidden her from working as a volunteer at the local hospital, and she was sure he would not allow her to visit a notoriously rough area of the city to work with disadvantaged youths.

It was that word 'allow' that infuriated her, she brooded as the taxi crept along at snail's pace. She understood his concerns for the baby, but she was an adult who could make her own decisions. After her phone call to Father Thomaso she had been determined to visit the youth centre and meet some of the young people he was trying to support. But she knew that Stavros would immediately report back to Nikos, and so she had asked him to take her to the museum, knowing that he could be persuaded to wait in the car for her rather than be dragged around the exhibit rooms.

Once Stavros had left her, she had slipped out of a side door and hailed a taxi to take her across town. The hours she had spent with Father Thomaso had convinced her that she had finally found something worthwhile to do with her empty days while Nikos was at work. But she knew she could not continue to deceive Nikos. On the journey back across town she wondered how she could convince him that she would come to no harm working at the youth centre—but when the taxi finally drew up outside the museum her heart sank at the sight of him standing, grim-faced, with Stavros.

Okay, she shouldn't have gone behind his back, she owned when she stepped out of the taxi. She owed him an apology and an explanation, but she hadn't broken any laws, and there was no reason why he should be looking at her with such icy fury that her blood ran cold.

'Stavros is in no way to blame,' she said quietly when she reached him. 'I sent him away, but I can explain.'

'Can you?' Nikos ground out, struggling to control the anger that had surged through him when he had seen her in the taxi and realised she had deliberately tricked her bodyguard. When Stavros had phoned him and explained that Kitty had disappeared from the museum, he had broken off his board meeting and raced across town, breaking every speed limit. Thoughts of kidnap had filled him with dread, but now a new fear churned in his gut. Where had she been? And why had she needed to go off in secret? He glanced round at Stavros and the security staff from the museum who had searched for her, and caught hold of Kitty's arm in a bruising grip that made her wince. 'We can't talk here,' he bit out tersely as he marched her over to his car and yanked open the door. 'Get in.'

Kitty knew better than to argue. His fury was palpable, and she quickly slid into her seat and stared straight ahead when he walked round the car and got in next to her. His silence during the journey back to the apartment shredded her nerves, and when she preceded him down the hall she was tempted to make a run for it and lock herself in her bathroom. She walked into the living room with him close behind her, and he immediately crossed to the bar, poured whisky into a glass and gulped it down. His tension was so fierce that even from a few feet away Kitty could feel it, and she felt a frisson of real fear when he strode towards her.

'Where have you been all day, Kitty?' His hand shot out and gripped her chin, holding her so tight that she was sure he would crush her jaw.

'Nikos…you're hurting me.' Tears filled her eyes, and she swayed, feeling sick. She suddenly remembered that she had missed lunch. She had been busy talking to one of the boys at the youth club who had run away from home after his abusive stepfather had beaten him. Time had passed as she had sat with Yanni and tried to comfort him, but now her blood sugars were low and she was afraid she was going to faint. 'Let go of me and I'll tell you,' she pleaded. 'For pity's sake, Nikos! You're scaring me, and this level of tension can't be good for the baby.'

'You mean there is still a baby?' he growled savagely. He flung her from him, and she stumbled, but he stood staring at her, his eyes so dark and bitter that she shook her head in bewilderment.

'Of course there's still a baby. Why wouldn't there be?' she faltered.

'You tell me, Kitty. This morning you told me how much you hate being pregnant, and then later you gave Stavros the slip and went off without telling anyone where you were going. But maybe you didn't want anyone to know,' he snarled. 'Maybe you went to a private clinic and dealt with the problem of your pregnancy.'

Either she was crazy, or he was. 'What clinic?' she demanded desperately. 'There isn't a problem with my pregnancy. I don't understand what you mean, Nikos.' She kept replaying his words in her head, and slowly, slowly, they made an appalling kind of sense. *Dealt with the problem of your pregnancy!* Her knees sagged and she dropped down onto the sofa. 'You can't mean…you can't think…' She felt as though an iron band were tightening around her chest, squeezing the oxygen from her lungs. 'You can't think that I would—' she could hardly bring herself to utter the words '—get rid of the baby?'

'Why not?' His eyes were black and dead. 'It's what my first wife did.'

'*No.*' What he was telling her was too terrible to comprehend, and she closed her eyes, feeling utterly incapable of dealing with the pain that ravaged his face. 'You must be wrong,' she said jerkily. 'Surely your wife wouldn't have done that...*I* wouldn't do that,' she said in a stronger voice as she got unsteadily to her feet and crossed the room towards him. He stood immovable and grim-faced, and she saw him tense in rejection when she came close. But she did not care. Nothing mattered except that he should understand their child was safe.

She took his hand and held it over her stomach, and stared up at him, her eyes locked with his. 'Our baby is here inside me, and only fate will decide if it will be born safe and well in seven months' time. But I will do my best to nurture and protect it, and I would never, ever do anything to harm it. Please, Nikos, you must believe me,' she said shakily when he remained still and cold as a marble statue. 'I didn't say I hated being pregnant this morning.' Colour stained her pale face as she remembered how she had been ill in front of him. 'I meant that I hated being sick while you were there. I was... embarrassed for you to see me like that. Morning sickness isn't very glamorous,' she muttered.

At last he moved, as if blood once more ran in his veins rather than ice. 'You could not help being sick,' he said harshly. He stared at his hand on her stomach, and curved his fingers slightly as if he could somehow cradle the child within her. Slowly he lifted his eyes to her face and felt a jolt of shock when he saw her tears falling in a silent stream down her cheeks. 'I thought—' He broke off. 'You were so miserable this morning, and you seemed to resent being pregnant. When I learned from Stavros that you had disappeared, and then realised the lengths you had taken to get away from him, I believed there could only be one reason why you would make such an elaborate deceit. My past experience coloured my judgement, and I jumped to the wrong conclusion,' he said stiffly. He took his hand from her stomach and swung away to stare bleakly out over the city. 'Forgive me.'

His tone told her that he did not care whether she did or not.

Kitty stared at his rigid shoulders, and bit her lip, wondering if she dared voice the questions circling in her head. 'Did your first wife really…?'

'Abort my child?' He finished the question for her, his voice now flat and utterly devoid of emotion. 'Yes.' He had never spoken of it before, but he suddenly found the words spilling from him. 'I had told Greta of my family history and she knew I would never abandon my child as my father had done. I don't know if Greta's pregnancy was a genuine mistake, or if she missed her contraceptive Pill deliberately, but when I learned she was expecting my baby I immediately offered to marry her.

'I was devastated when she told me soon after

our marriage that she had suffered a miscarriage,' he continued grimly. 'She knew I wanted the child, but I discovered later that she had set her sights on marrying a millionaire, and once she had achieved her goal the child was no longer necessary. When our marriage crumbled because of her drug addiction, and she knew I intended to divorce her, she wanted to hurt me, and she told me that she had had an abortion.'

No wonder his heart was buried beneath impenetrable layers of granite, Kitty thought, aching with sadness for him. She wanted to wrap her arms around him and simply hold him, but she knew he would reject her, and now she understood why. His trust and faith in humanity had not just been shattered, but utterly and cruelly destroyed beyond repair.

'Where is Greta now?' she asked huskily.

'She died two years ago as a result of her drug habit.'

There was not a shred of pity in his voice. He had stated that he had married his first wife after she conceived his baby, but Kitty knew instinctively that it had been more than that. Had he loved her? She was startled by how much the idea hurt, and she pushed her ridiculous jealousy away. If he had cared for Greta, then her betrayal must have been doubly agonising.

She understood now why he wanted his child so

desperately. He had lost his only blood relative when he was a vulnerable teenager, and later suffered the most terrible betrayal by his first wife. The baby inside her meant everything to him, and she knew then that whatever happened between them in the future—even if they ended up rowing constantly—she could never separate him from his child.

But she could not contemplate a time when she might want to end their marriage. She loved him, Kitty admitted silently. From the very beginning she had been drawn to him by more than just the sexual chemistry that burned between them. She had thought he was cold and heartless, but how could he be anything else after the pain he had suffered in his life? She wished she could go to him and tell him that she would always be there for him. But he did not want her love, and she did not want to burden him with it or make him feel guilty that he could never love her in return.

She was at a loss to know what to say to him, and even though he was standing only a few feet away the distance between them seemed un-bridgeable. Tiredness rolled over her in a wave, and with it a feeling of defeat. After all he had suffered he would never lower his guard and feel normal emotions like trust and caring. When they had married he'd told her bluntly that he would never love her, and she had accepted it. But it hadn't stopped her secretly hoping that over time their physical relationship would develop into something more. Now she knew there was no hope of that ever happening. His emotional scars ran too deep and she could not blame him for refusing to risk being hurt again.

Nikos was staring unseeingly out of the window, lost in his bitter memories, but he suddenly swung round and pierced her with a sharp stare. 'So, where did you go today?'

Kitty took a deep breath, ashamed of her stupid deceit now that she knew how badly he had been deceived in the past. 'I went to visit a youth centre for underprivileged children and teenagers. I read about it in the newspaper, and remembered the priest who runs it, Father Thomaso, from Aristo.

'I know I should have told you, Nikos, but I was afraid you would stop me. You have no idea what terrible lives some of those children have had,' she said urgently. 'I've spent my whole life as a pampered princess, and I want to do something useful and meaningful. I know I can give money, but what the children really need is someone to listen to them, someone to care—'

She broke off, not encouraged by his frown, and fully expecting him to accuse her of putting the baby at risk, but his reaction surprised her.

'Actually I know only too well from my own childhood experiences what their lives are like,' he said quietly, staring at her intently as he tried to understand her. She was a princess from one of the wealthiest families in Europe, yet despite her privileged upbringing she wanted to help the poor and desperate who lived on the streets. None of the women he had ever dated in his past had had a social conscience, and he didn't know quite what to make of her.

'I told you that I inherited Petridis Shipping from Larissa.' He broke the silence that had fallen between them. 'But I did not want Larissa's personal fortune, I was determined to make my own, and so I put her money into a charitable fund which provides financial support to a number of causes, including, as it happens, the youth centre you visited today. I have never met Father Thomaso, but I know of his work and I have already organised for Larissa's charitable fund to make a significant donation to his centre.'

Something flared in his eyes, a new respect for her that lifted her heart. 'I don't think you should take on too many commitments while you are pregnant, and after the baby is born you will be busy. But I am looking for someone to become president of the charitable fund I've set up. The position is yours, if you want it.'

He walked over to her when she eagerly nodded her head, and slid his hand beneath her chin, tilting her face to him. 'We married for the sake of our child, and if I'm honest I believed you were as shallow as the women I dated before I met you,' he said bluntly. 'But you constantly surprise me, Kitty,' he finished, his frustration that he did not understand her tangible. He was shocked that he had revealed so much of himself to her, but to his surprise he realised that he did not regret telling her about his past. After Greta, he had believed he would never trust anyone, but when he looked into Kitty's soft, brown eyes he felt...*healed.*

He looked down at her pale face and frowned when she swayed unsteadily on her feet. 'What's wrong?' he demanded sharply. 'Are you ill?'

'I forgot lunch,' she admitted sheepishly. 'And now I feel sick again and I don't think I can manage dinner.'

'Kitty! Do you think you could worry about other people a bit less, and yourself a bit more?' he growled, ignoring her startled gasp as he swung her into his arms and strode down the hall.

'I'm sorry,' she mumbled, trying to resist the urge to press her face into his neck and breathe in his tantalising male scent. 'I know you're concerned for the baby.'

'Actually, *agape*, I am concerned about you.' She looked drained and infinitely fragile, and something indefinable tugged at his heart, but he forced it away and reminded himself that she was the mother of his child and so of course he cared about her welfare.

He stopped off at the kitchen and stood over her until she had forced down a banana and a glass of milk. Then he carried her to the bedroom—as if she were as light as a feather rather than a well-built, pregnant woman, Kitty mused sleepily as he removed her clothes and slipped a nightdress over her head before he helped her into bed. She was asleep within seconds of her head touching the pillow, but Nikos lay awake long into the night, his thoughts preoccupied—not by his past, but his future with the woman lying beside him.

CHAPTER TWELVE

KITTY smoothed a crease from the skirt of her elegant cream linen suit, and skimmed through her notes one last time. Around her, the hotel banqueting room was filled with guests who were attending the lunch in support of the youth centre Father Thomaso had set up—and in her role as patron of the charity, she was about to give a speech outlining the aims of the centre and asking for donations.

Beside her, Nikos smiled and rested his hand lightly on her thigh. 'Are you nervous, *agape?* There must be several hundred people here today.'

Kitty took a deep breath, and squared her shoulders. 'I'm fine,' she said confidently, ignoring the few butterflies in her stomach. She knew that once she walked onto the stage, and began to talk about the centre and the lives of the children it aimed to support, her nerves would disappear.

It seemed hard to believe that only a short

while ago she had been so crippled by shyness that any type of socialising had been an ordeal. Since she had married Nikos and moved to Athens she felt as though she had emerged from a shell. She was no longer drab, dumpy Kitty Karedes. She knew she looked good in the clothes he bought her, and the admiration in his eyes made her feel more confident about her curvy figure.

'Are you sure? You look a little flushed,' Nikos murmured, his eyes glinting wickedly as his hand inched higher up her skirt.

'Will you behave—at least until later, when we're alone?' Kitty choked, amusement and desire mingling as she prised his hand from her leg. 'You have an insatiable appetite, Nikos.'

'Only for you, Kitty *mou*,' he drawled lazily. The sensual promise in his eyes caused the familiar weakness in Kitty's limbs, and she wished they were back home at the apartment and he would spend the rest of the afternoon making love to her. But first she had a speech to give, and then they were going to the hospital for her first antenatal scan. Up on stage the event organiser announced her name, and she gathered up her notes.

'Wish me luck,' she murmured, and gave a startled gasp when he leaned towards her and claimed her mouth in a slow, sweet kiss.

'You don't need luck—you're a brilliant

speaker.' He paused and then said quietly, 'I am very proud of you, *agape*.'

She blushed and gave one of her soft smiles that tugged at Nikos's insides before she walked up the room, and when she stepped onto the stage he joined the other guests and applauded her, feeling a mixture of pride and frustration that just lately she seemed to dominate his thoughts to the exclusion of anything else.

Ever since the day she had visited Father Thomaso's youth centre, and the explosive confrontation that had followed, which had led him to telling her about his past, a fragile bond had developed between them. The last few weeks had been… good, he admitted, refusing to dwell on the fact that he had cut back significantly on his working hours so that he could spend time with her. It was important that they established a friendly relationship before the baby was born, but he was surprised and faintly dismayed by how much he enjoyed her company.

Kitty was no longer the wary and reserved person she had been when he had first brought her to Athens, and since he had appointed her as head of the Larissa Petridis Foundation her confidence had soared. She took her charity work seriously and the media had dubbed her the Caring Princess. She had become something of a celebrity in Athens, and even he was privately amazed by her transformation from a shy, reluctant royal to a graceful and breathtakingly beautiful princess.

Without him being aware of her doing it, she had encouraged him to talk about the issues that still haunted him, in particular his feeling that he had failed to protect his first child. Thanks to Kitty he was slowly coming to terms with his past, and he was looking forward to the future when he would be a father. But although he trusted her in a way he had never believed he would trust any human being, he couldn't shake off the feeling that she was holding back from him, particularly when he made love to her, and that in turn made him reluctant to lower his guard.

The press were waiting for them when they emerged from the hotel. Kitty did not enjoy their constant attention, but she dealt with it with quiet dignity, smiling and standing with Nikos's arm around her waist while the photographers jostled to take pictures.

'At least it will bring the youth centre to every-one's notice,' she murmured when they finally made it to the car and Stavros sped off. But she was glad they had lost the paparazzi by the time they reached the hospital. The scan was a private matter for her and Nikos and she didn't want to share the experience with the rest of the world.

Inside the private hospital they walked along

plush carpeted corridors to the obstetrician's office. 'Dr Antoniadis is the best in Greece,' Nikos had told her when he had made the appointment. 'He will oversee your care and personally deliver the baby.' Nothing, it seemed, was too good for Nikos's child.

Dr Antoniadis carried out some basic checks on Kitty and then chatted to them both about the type of birth she hoped to have.

'Painless, hopefully,' she quipped, feeling a sudden rush of nerves when she thought about the technicalities of giving birth. To her surprise, Nikos reached across and clasped her hand.

'I will be with you every minute of your labour,' he promised. And for some reason the strength in his voice and the firmness of his fingers gripping hers made Kitty want to cry. Fortunately a nurse appeared and led her off to change into a hospital gown, ready for the scan, and then, when she lay on the bed in the scanning room and someone smeared cold jelly over her, she was more concerned with the size of her stomach, which was already discernibly rounded, to give much thought to anything else.

'You won't see much at this early stage,' the technician explained as a fuzzy grey blur appeared on the screen. 'We really just want to check the heartbeat—and there it is. Can you see it? That little pulse there is your baby.'

Kitty stared at the screen, at the indistinct blob of cells and the tiny but plainly visible speck that was beating rhythmically, and emotion flooded through her. In that moment her pregnancy became real. It was no longer something vague: a line on a pregnancy kit and nausea in the mornings. A human life was developing inside her: her child—hers and Nikos's. She blinked to dispel the moisture that had welled in her eyes, and turned to him. And more tears gathered when she saw his face. He was leaning forward slightly in his chair, staring intently at the grainy image, and she could see the tension in his shoulders, the absolute stillness, as if he were afraid that if he moved the picture on the screen would disappear.

'Nikos.' Her voice was choked, and he stirred then and gripped her hand, lifted it to his mouth and pressed his lips to her fingers.

'We will give our child everything,' he said rawly.

She knew he was thinking about his own childhood when he had had so little. 'Of course we will,' she assured him softly. 'But a child needs more than material things. A child needs love, perhaps more than anything—and we will love it—he or she,' she added with a smile as she pictured a little boy with dark hair and flashing eyes, or a girl with pink cheeks—probably chubby cheeks if the baby took after her, she thought ruefully.

Afterwards they strolled around the park next

to the hospital, where the late afternoon sunshine filtered through the leaves of the cypress trees and made patterns of gold on the paths.

'What do you hope it is—a boy or a girl?' she asked curiously.

'I don't know.' Nikos looked startled for a moment, as if it was the first time he had considered that the baby would be one or the other. 'I don't mind,' he said seriously, echoing her own thoughts, and she glanced at him and shared the unspoken message that what really mattered was that their child would be healthy and born safely.

'It's exciting, isn't it—to think that in a few months from now the baby will actually be here?' Kitty felt her heart flip as she imagined cradling her child in her arms. Since the scan she couldn't stop smiling. Her pregnancy had been unplanned and a huge shock, but she did not regret it, and she couldn't wait to be a mother.

'Yes, it's exciting.' Nikos returned her smile and slipped his hand into hers as they walked. Their child would form a bond between them that would last a lifetime, Kitty realised, loving the new closeness she sensed was developing between them.

'Tell me about your childhood,' he said suddenly. 'I've told you about mine, but yours must have been very different, growing up in a palace with the other members of the royal family.'

'Well, I certainly never wanted for anything,' she murmured. 'The palace was an amazing place to grow up, although of course when I was a child I didn't realise how privileged I was. But it wasn't just material things. There were five of us children, so I was never lonely. And although my parents were busy much of the time with state affairs, they always had time for us.

'I was especially close to my father,' she revealed with a soft smile as she remembered the late king. 'I adored him. When I was a little girl he used to come to the nursery every night and read stories from my favourite book—*Russian Fairy Tales and Fables*.' Kitty's smile faded and she felt the familiar pang of sadness that she would never see her father again, or hear his deep, rumbling tones. 'He used to tell me that I would grow up to be a beautiful princess like in the fairy tales, and that one day I would marry a handsome prince.'

But in fairy tales the prince always fell in love with the princess—which just went to show the difference between fantasy fiction and real life, she thought bleakly as she stared at Nikos's sculpted features and saw the inherent toughness in the hard line of his jaw.

'I wish I still had the book,' she said wistfully. 'Unfortunately it was lost in a fire that destroyed part of the palace nursery a few years ago. It's out of print now, and the few copies that exist are owned by private collectors, so I don't suppose I'll ever be able to read it to our child.'

'We'll buy new books, and toys—everything the baby needs,' Nikos murmured, thinking of his own childhood that had lacked even basic necessities such as food, let alone toys and books. Kitty had said that a child needed love more than material possessions, and maybe she was right. He knew without doubt that he would love his child, but what kind of father would he be when he had never had a role model? He felt singularly inadequate for the job, especially when Kitty would surely compare his efforts at fatherhood with her own father, whom she had obviously idolised.

Her life had turned out vastly different from the life she must have imagined as a child, he brooded. Instead of meeting a prince with an aristocratic lineage she had been forced to marry a commoner who had no idea who had fathered him. And she missed Aristo and the royal palace—she never said so, but he knew she didn't enjoy living in the apartment in the centre of a busy city, and that when he was at work she often visited Athens' famous National Gardens.

'Maybe we should start looking at houses,' he startled Kitty by saying. 'Somewhere in the suburbs, with a garden for the baby to play in when it's older. Would you like that?'

'It would be nice,' she replied slowly. 'But you like the apartment. It's your bachelor pad.'

'Mmm, but I am not a bachelor any more, and I want what is best for our child—I'll contact some estate agents,' Nikos said decisively. 'But moving takes time, and for now I was thinking that we could turn your dressing room into a nursery so that we are close to the baby if it wakes during the night—unless you're planning on sleeping in there again yourself?'

Kitty blushed at the teasing glint in his eyes, knowing that he was remembering her first few nights at the apartment when she had refused to share his bed. 'You might prefer us to sleep apart when I'm nine months pregnant and the size of a whale,' she murmured, voicing the fear that had been niggling away at her that he would no longer find her attractive when she was heavily pregnant. 'Really, Nikos, I'm sure I'm going to be *huge*. I've already gained weight.'

'I know,' he growled as he leaned against a tree and drew her into his arms. 'Your breasts are bigger—and I am definitely a breast man,' he muttered, deftly unbuttoning her jacket so that he could caress her full curves that were straining beneath her silk blouse. He ran his finger lightly down her cheek and saw the betraying quiver that ran through her. 'You look tired, *agape*.'

'Oh!' Kitty's face fell. She did not want to be

told she looked tired; she wanted Nikos to tell her she looked gorgeous and sexy and that he was impatient to take her to bed. 'Well, I'm not. I feel fine.'

'What a pity.' His mouth curved into an amused smile when she stared at him in confusion. 'I was thinking that you should spend the rest of the afternoon lying down—and to prevent you from feeling bored, I would lie with you and…entertain you.'

Kitty couldn't restrain the little shiver of excitement that ran through her, and she felt a delicious tingle of anticipation at the sultry gleam in Nikos's eyes. 'In that case, we'd better go home,' she whispered against his mouth, and gave a low murmur of approval when he claimed her lips in a hungry kiss that demanded her eager response.

Fortunately it was not far back to the apartment, although Nikos was so impatient that he had already removed her jacket and unfastened her blouse by the time the lift reached the top floor.

'You mustn't keep carrying me,' she protested when he swept her into his arms and raced down the hall. 'I'm no lightweight, Nikos.'

He laughed, and the sound rumbled in his big chest as he lowered her to her feet in the bedroom. 'I like carrying you. You fit into my arms,' he murmured, tugging her blouse over her shoulders and reaching round to unsnap her bra.

Her breasts were getting huge, and her nipples were bigger and darker, Kitty noted dismally when she glanced down. She looked so different from the skinny, flat-chested blonde models Nikos had dated in the past, and some of her old insecurity about her shape returned. Sunshine was pouring through the windows, and she was unnerved at the thought of taking off her clothes and standing stark naked in the brilliant light, when before they had only ever made love in the soft glow from the bedside lamps.

'I'll shut the blinds,' she murmured, inching away from him and crossing her arms over her breasts.

His brows rose quizzically and he paused in the act of removing his shirt. 'Why? We're on the top floor and not overlooked by anyone,' he said, the amusement in his voice fading when he tried to prise her arms open and she stubbornly resisted. 'What's the matter, Kitty? Why don't you like me seeing your body? Don't think I haven't noticed that you hide beneath the sheets whenever you can.'

His strength easily outmatched hers, and Kitty hung her head when he drew her arms down to her sides. 'I'm fat,' she burst out miserably. 'And it's not all due to being pregnant. I've always had curves, and I've never liked my body—not since—' She broke off and stared determinedly at the carpet.

Frowning, Nikos put a finger under her chin and tilted her face up. 'Not since what, *agape?*'

She shrugged awkwardly, sure that Nikos must be growing impatient with her. But when she looked at him she saw nothing but concern in his dark eyes, and she felt a sudden urge to confide in him.

'It's stupid, really,' she muttered. 'I went on a date years ago. My first date as it happens. My father had always been very protective, and I was ridiculously naïve. Anyway, my father persuaded me to go on a date with the son of one of his friends—I think Papa probably arranged it because he'd realised I was never going to find a boyfriend when I spent all my time in the library,' she told Nikos wryly.

'The evening was a disaster, culminating in my "date" assaulting me in the back of his car.'

'What do you mean by *assaulted*? Were you raped?' Nikos was shocked by the savage anger that coursed through him, and the surge of protectiveness that made him want to pull Kitty into his arms and simply hold her.

'No, no,' she assured him quickly. 'To be honest, I think he was too drunk. But he ripped my dress and…and touched me, and when I tried to stop him, he accused me of leading him on. He made me feel ashamed of my body, and I suppose I let the incident grow huge in my mind.

'When I met you, and we made love in the cave,

I was pretending to be somebody else, and I forgot all my inhibitions…' She trailed off and stared at Nikos, and then said rather desperately, 'I really would be happier if we shut the blinds.'

He shook his head, and reached for her, drawing her gently against him so that her breasts were crushed against his chest while he threaded his fingers through her hair. 'Who was this friend of the family who violated you and shattered your self-confidence?' he demanded.

Kitty hesitated. 'Vasilis Sarondakos.'

'*Theos*! Sarondakos again! Pray for his sake that I never run into him, because my fist is itching to meet his face,' Nikos said grimly. 'But there are more subtle methods of retribution. I happen to know that Vasilis has spent the fortune he inherited from his grandfather and is desperately looking for a backer for his business venture. Wouldn't it be a pity if he failed to get the cash he needs?' he murmured with a cold gleam in his eyes that warned Kitty he would be a dangerous opponent in the boardroom. 'I'll call in a few favours with my banking friends.' He smiled at her, warmth replacing the icy anger that he felt for Vasilis.

'Forget Sarondakos and his spite, *agape*. You should be proud of your gorgeous body, not want to hide it away. Do you feel dirty or ashamed when I make love to you?' he asked softly.

Slowly, Kitty shook her head, afraid that if she admitted she felt nothing but desperate, searing desire when she was in his arms he would realise the effect he had on her.

He was stroking her hair, soothing the tension from her, and her heart missed a beat when he eased her away from him a fraction and cradled her breasts in his hands. 'I want to see the sunlight gild your body when I make love to you,' he said, his voice as soft and sensuous as crushed velvet. 'I want to watch your eyes darken when I touch you like this.' He brushed his thumb pads over her nipples and then rolled the taut peaks between his fingers, sending exquisite sensation shooting through her. 'And I want to see all of you, Kitty, every last delectable inch.'

Her skirt fluttered to the floor, and she heard him inhale sharply as his gaze roamed over her gossamer-fine stockings and stiletto heels, and the tiny scrap of white lace that covered her femininity. Her thick chestnut hair had fallen forwards, and he pushed it back over her shoulders and cupped her breasts again, his eyes gleaming hotly beneath his heavy lids.

'*Theos*, how can you doubt what you do to me?' he demanded rawly as his restraint gave way and he hauled her into his arms so that the throbbing force of his arousal pushed insistently between her thighs. He claimed her mouth in a fierce, hungry kiss, and somehow managed to strip out of his clothes and push her backwards onto the bed without taking his lips from hers.

In the sunlight his hair gleamed like black satin as he moved down her body, pausing to take each swollen nipple into his mouth while he dipped his hand between her thighs. She was wet and ready for him and arched her hips in mute supplication as he caressed her. He withdrew his finger and pushed her legs wider apart and she thought he would take her immediately, and her breathing quickened. Instead she gave a shocked cry when he bent his head and placed his mouth over her femininity, his tongue taking the place of his finger as he thrust it into her damp opening.

'Nikos…no!' Frantic with embarrassment she gripped his hair and tried to drag his head up, but he did not cease his intimate caress and soon she forgot everything but the molten heat of her desire and her spiralling need for his full possession. Just when she thought she could withstand no more, and teetered on the edge of orgasm, he moved over her and entered her with one forceful thrust, his erection so powerful that he had to pause while her muscles stretched to accommodate him. And then he moved again, quick and hard, each sure stroke building her pleasure until it was unbearable and she could feel the first spasms pulsate deep in her pelvis.

She almost cried out as wave after wave of sensation ripped through her, but some deep-held instinct for self-protection made her stifle her moans, and she closed her eyes so that he would not see the depth of her emotions as they climaxed simultaneously. He was the love of her life, she thought when they lay together while their breathing gradually slowed. After the incredible passion they had just shared it seemed impossible that he did not feel something for her, some small glimmer of affection that would give hope to her starving heart.

But when he rolled off her and gave a languorous stretch, his satisfied smile was that of a man who had just enjoyed fantastic sex that had left his body sated and his emotions untouched. He got up from the bed, and her eyes were drawn helplessly to him, her stomach dipping as she absorbed the masculine beauty of his lean, hard body, gleaming like bronze in the afternoon sunlight. She thought he was heading for the en suite, but he carried on out of the bedroom, returning minutes later with a slim velvet box in his hands.

'I bought you a present,' he murmured as he rejoined her on the bed.

'Another one?' she protested faintly, thinking of the numerous dresses, exotic underwear, and fabulous jewellery he had given her over the past few weeks. If he only knew it, she would swap all of them for the words she longed to hear from him. But she knew he would never say them. She was his wife, and the mother of his child, but she was not the love of his life, and she never would be. It was just a pity her aching heart could not accept that fact.

'Aren't you going to open it?'

Quickly she flipped open the box and stared at the necklace made up of dozens of square-cut diamonds that glittered like teardrops on the black velvet cushion. It was breathtaking, and, from her knowledge of jewellery from the Royal Collection on Aristo, mind-bogglingly expensive.

He was waiting for her to say something, but for some reason she wanted to cry and she bit down hard on her lip, her eyes blurring so that the diamonds seemed to fracture into a thousand sparkling shards. 'It's beautiful,' she choked, 'but you've already given me so much.' And yet of the things that mattered, so little. 'You don't have to keep buying me presents, Nikos.'

He lifted the necklace from the box and fastened it around her neck so that it lay cold against her skin. 'I like to buy you gifts,' he said with a shrug. 'I want you to know that I appreciate you.'

'Do you?' she asked cautiously, her heart trembling with fragile hope.

'Certainly.' His mouth curved into a sensual smile as he leaned back on the pillows to admire the diamonds at her throat. They had cost him the earth, but they were worth every penny when they were displayed in all their shimmering glory on her naked skin. 'Our marriage was not what either of us would have chosen,' he stated coolly, 'but we both acknowledge the responsibility we have towards the baby we created during a moment of madness. I think we have become friends as well as lovers, haven't we, Kitty? And I believe that our companionable relationship, based on mutual respect and trust, is the greatest gift we can give our child.'

Was that the reason he had made the effort to spend time with her—to befriend her and make her trust him? Was it all for the baby's sake? Of course it was, she acknowledged painfully. Their child would grow up in a harmonious environment with two parents who were polite and courteous towards each other as all good friends were. It should be enough. It would have to be enough. But it wasn't, and the loveless future that stretched before her suddenly seemed very bleak.

CHAPTER THIRTEEN

Nikos felt the last spasms slowly drain from his body, and rested his head on Kitty's breasts. Her skin was velvet soft beneath his cheek and he inhaled the delicate, floral scent of her perfume. He was tempted to remain lying on top of her, their bodies joined, but after a few moments he rolled over and stared up at the ceiling, feeling the familiar frustration that, although sex with her seemed to get better and better, the distance he sensed between them was growing wider.

He did not like clingy women, he reminded himself irritably. He should be pleased that Kitty no longer cuddled up to him after sex and instead moved to her side of the bed as soon as their passion was spent, but perversely he wished that she were not quite so unmoved by their physical intimacy.

He propped up on one elbow as she swung her legs over the side of the bed. At least she was no longer shy about her body, and did not rush to cover up, he mused as he studied her voluptuous breasts and delightfully round bottom, and felt himself harden again. He knew he should have no complaints about their marriage. They got on well out of bed, and their sex life was amazing. So why did he feel as though something was missing—something elusive, that he did not understand, but seemed to be the cause of the curious flatness he felt inside?

She had been brushing her hair, and now it rippled down her back like a river of silk. 'I thought we could host a dinner party next week,' she murmured as she set down the brush and turned to face him. 'We've been invited to several recently, and it's time we returned the compliment.'

'Fine—but it can't be next week,' he replied, thinking of the meeting that had been arranged at the last minute. 'I'm flying to New York on Sunday night and I'll be away until the following weekend.'

Kitty felt a stab of disappointment, and her voice was unwittingly sharp when she spoke. 'This is the first I've heard of your business trip.' She paused, and then added, 'I assume it is for business?' Shannon Marsh lived in New York. Was he planning on a reunion to catch up on old times? She instantly dismissed the idea. She trusted Nikos; he had married her because he wanted his child, and for the same reason he would remain faithful to her.

But she did not want him to go away. They had been getting on well recently, better than she had ever dared hope at the start of their marriage, and she was afraid that while he was away he might revert back to the old, cold Nikos. She wished he would suggest that she accompanied him to America, but maybe he thought she was too busy with her charity work? She hesitated, feeling a rush of nerves, and then murmured, 'Perhaps I could come with you?'

'Not this time, I'm afraid.'

His smile was meant to take the sting out of the words, but when all was said and done it was still a rejection, Kitty thought miserably.

'I'll be busy all week, and you'll get bored.' He saw the flare of hurt in her eyes and briefly contemplated changing his mind. But these were important negotiations, and she would be a distraction. If he was honest, the real reason he didn't want her with him was because he wanted some time to himself, Nikos acknowledged. She was in his mind a lot lately, more than he was comfortable with, and he needed to prove to himself that he could walk away from her any time he liked.

'Well—' Kitty dredged up a smile and tried to act as if it was no big deal '—another time, maybe?' But she was so hurt that she couldn't help being cool with him for the rest of the weekend, and he either didn't notice, or didn't care, because he made no comment when she turned away from him in bed on Saturday night, and, instead of pulling her into his arms as she longed for him to do, he rolled over and fell asleep, unaware that she wept silent tears into her pillow.

She had to stop this, Kitty told herself at the beginning of the following week—after she had bade Nikos a frosty goodbye and he had shrugged carelessly and walked out of the apartment without a backward glance. She had to stop longing for what he could never give her, and make the most of what she had—a charming, attentive, extremely virile husband who she knew was determined to make their marriage work.

But the days without him dragged, and although she kept herself busy with her work for the foundation she missed him desperately. He phoned every evening, but their conversations were stilted. The distance between them had nothing to do with the fact that they were miles apart; there was a subtle change in their relationship, and she was afraid she was losing the tenuous closeness she had sensed had grown between them.

But what was she expecting from him? she asked herself towards the end of the week, when his absence sat like a dull weight in her chest. She knew his history, and understood how terribly he had been damaged by his past. It was possible that he would never fully recover, yet she was still waiting for him to act like a knight in shining armour from the fairy tales she used to read, and go down on bended knee to proclaim his undying love for her.

Unlike him she had enjoyed a blissfully happy childhood surrounded by love from her parents, brothers and sister. It was easy for her to love when she had never known pain and rejection. But instead of telling him honestly how she felt about him, she hugged her love for him to herself like a miser, and hid her emotions behind her pride.

Perhaps it was time to dismiss her pride and ignore that little voice in her head that whispered that in love stories the hero had to admit his love first. This wasn't a story, this was real life—and Nikos's life had been far from a fairy tale. The worst he could do would be to tell her that he would never love her in return, she told herself, feeling a flutter of fear in her stomach at that very likely prospect. Since he had married her he had shown her kindness and respect, and his faith in her ability to head the charitable foundation he had set up in honour of the woman who had befriended him had been a huge boost to her self-confidence.

Lost in her thoughts, she did not notice that Sotiri had come out onto the terrace with her breakfast until he halted by the table and gave a low whistle.

'Anastasia!'

Kitty followed his gaze to the portrait of Nikos's mother that had been delivered to the apartment that morning and was now propped on a chair. 'Was that her name? I didn't realise you knew her, Sotiri.'

'Sure thing—Nikos and I grew up on the same streets. His mother was a lovely lady; everyone liked her. It broke Nikos's heart when she died,' Sotiri said gruffly. 'Where did you get the painting?'

'I took a copy of the little photo on his desk and sent it to an artist on Aristo who has painted all the recent portraits of the royal family,' Kitty explained. 'Nikos had told me that the photo was his only memento of his mother, and I thought it would be nice to have a proper painting of her. The artist has done a good job and caught her likeness perfectly,' she murmured as she studied the painting. 'I was planning to give it to Nikos when he arrives home on Sunday—which I also happen to know is his birthday, although he hasn't mentioned it. Do you think he'll like it, Sotiri?' she queried, doubts forming when he continued to stare at the picture with a curious expression on his face.

He turned to her and gave her an intent glance. 'I think he'll be speechless, Miss Kitty.' He hesitated and then said quietly, 'He does have a heart, you know; he just keeps it well hidden.'

Kitty spent the whole of Sunday torn between excitement because Nikos would soon be home and dread because he might not like the painting, or her reason for giving it to him. She had learned from his secretary that his flight was due to land in Athens late in the afternoon. Sotiri had prepared a special dinner, and had left it ready for her to serve, and she set the table, added candles and flowers and placed the wrapped portrait on his chair.

After a long debate over what to wear she chose a simple gold silk gown, which was cleverly cut to disguise the pregnancy weight she'd gained on her hips and stomach, and had a low-cut neckline that she knew Nikos would approve of. She left her hair loose, the way he liked it, put on the diamond necklace that had been his last gift to her, and sprayed perfume to her pulse points, and then paced the apartment impatiently, her heart thudding.

But he didn't come home. As the evening ticked by her tension grew, and finally, when it seemed unlikely that his flight would be this late, she phoned his mobile.

'Angelaki,' he answered just as she was about to cut the call, and she frowned at the background sounds of music and female voices.

'Nikos, I was expecting you home hours ago.'

'Were you?' He sounded dismissive and vaguely surprised. 'I don't remember saying what time I would be home.'

'No, but I thought…' She trailed off. 'Are you back in Athens? Where are you?'

'The casino—I bumped into a couple of friends at the airport.' A woman laughed close to the phone. No doubt she was some blonde bimbo who was hanging onto his arm, waiting for him to finish his call to his wife, Kitty thought furiously. 'Don't wait up for me, *agape*. I could be a while.'

'Fine.' Her hands were shaking when she ended the call, and tears burned her eyes. She had spent the whole week looking forward to him coming home, but he couldn't have emphasised more clearly that he hadn't given her a second thought while he had been away, and was in no rush to see her again.

He had never given any indication that he wanted her to be anything more than his convenient sex partner and the mother of his child, she reminded herself bleakly. It was not his fault that she had fallen in love with him, and he would be astonished if he could see her now, with tears and mascara streaking her face as she threw herself on the bed and cried until her heart ached.

Nothing much had changed, Nikos brooded as he glanced around the casino. It was the same old crowd of die-hard bachelors grouped around the roulette table, the same vacuous girls flirting with any rich-looking man under seventy. This had been his way of life for years and he had never questioned whether or not he enjoyed it, he thought as he detached himself from a predatory blonde and walked towards the exit.

He didn't know why he had come here. But that was a lie, he acknowledged, raking a hand through his hair. He had come because he was scared to go home. Him—Nikos Angelaki—the toughest kid on the streets, the most feared adversary in the boardroom. He had known this churning feeling in his gut before; when he'd sat with his mother in the hospital and vowed he would earn the money somehow for her cancer treatment, and she had smiled her soft smile at him and said it was too late. He'd felt that same sickening sensation in his gut when he'd looked at Greta, spaced out on cocaine, and realised she was telling him the truth about his baby.

But this was a different feeling, and it had been gnawing away at him all week while he had been in the States missing Kitty so badly that he had only felt half alive. He had been blind for weeks, or maybe so afraid of what he could see that he had closed his eyes and ignored it. He couldn't ignore it any longer—or avoid her, he brooded as he stepped off the kerb and hailed a taxi. He didn't belong in the nightclubs and casinos; he belonged at home with his wife.

It was almost midnight when he walked into the apartment. He had expected it to be in darkness, and Kitty to have gone to bed, but a light glowed beneath the dining-room door. Frowning, he opened it, and stopped dead. Someone had taken great care with the table—but he doubted Sotiri had arranged the floral centrepiece or hung the birthday banner on the wall.

A faint noise from behind him told him he was no longer alone, and he jerked his head round to see Kitty standing in the doorway. She was wearing a shimmery gold dress that displayed a tantalising amount of her full breasts, and predictably desire surged through him. His gaze moved up to her face. Unusually she was wearing her glasses instead of her contacts, but he could see that her eyes were red-rimmed as if she had been crying.

'How was your trip?' she asked in a curiously flat voice.

'Successful.' He shrugged, unable to drum up much interest in the completion of a deal that a few months ago would have had him buzzing for days. He glanced back at the table. 'If I'd known you had planned for us to have dinner together I would have come home earlier.'

It was a fair point, Kitty admitted silently. But

she had been afraid to tell him of her plans for his birthday in case he rejected her. 'It's your birthday,' she murmured, 'and you have a right to spend it how you choose.'

He gave a faint laugh. 'I'd forgotten it was my birthday until I walked in and saw the banner. The last birthday I celebrated was my sixteenth, before my mother died.' He looked at the wrapped parcel. 'How did you know it was today?'

'I looked in your passport.' Kitty tried to imagine him at sixteen: a boy on the threshold of manhood who less than a year later had been left without a single relative in the world. She groped for courage and smiled at him. 'Are you going to open your present?' she asked softly.

Nikos did not know what he was expecting, or why his heart was jerking unevenly in his chest. He couldn't actually remember having a surprise birthday present in his life, and he didn't know how to react. Kitty was watching him, and after a moment's hesitation he ripped off the paper and stared in stunned silence at the portrait, feeling an unfamiliar stinging sensation behind his eyelids.

'Do you like it?' Kitty could not bear the taut silence. 'The artist worked from a copy of the photo of your mother. I think he's done a good job, don't you?'

'I...don't know what to say.' His throat felt raw as the emotions he had suppressed for so many years burned a fiery path inside him. It was many long years since the woman captured so perfectly on the canvas had smiled at him and told him that she loved him, but as Nikos stared at the image of his mother he felt his heart crack open.

'Nikos?' His frozen stillness was not the reaction Kitty had hoped for and for a terrible moment she thought he was angry. But then he looked over at her and she saw his wet lashes, and the tension that had gripped her for the past few hours when she had been waiting for him to come home snapped. 'Oh, Nikos—*don't*!'

She flew to him and touched his face with trembling fingers. 'I never meant to upset you.'

'You haven't.' He fought to control the emotions that were coursing through him like a relentless torrent released from a dam. 'It's a wonderful present, Kitty. I can't believe you went to so much trouble.' He looked again at the painting and his eyes ached. 'Why did you?'

'Because I know how much you loved her.' She took a deep breath, her heart beating liked a trapped bird beneath her ribs. 'And because I love *you*, Nikos. With all my heart.'

'Kitty!' He placed the painting carefully on the table and then turned back to her and gripped her upper arms so tightly that his fingers bit into her skin. Was he going to shake her until she retracted her last statement? she wondered, her heart turning over at the hunted expression on his face.

'It's all right,' she assured him gently. 'I know you don't feel the same way about me. I think you loved Greta, and I understand that after what she did you would never want to love anyone again.'

Tears blurred her vision and misted her glasses, and when she took them off she missed the flare of emotion in his eyes. 'I fell in love with you that night in the cave,' she told him, her voice steady and fearless, although inside she was shaking, 'and although I tried hard to deny my feelings, I know I will love you until I die.'

She wished he would say something, even if it was the words of rejection she was expecting, but he continued to stare at her as if he had never really seen her before, and his thoughts were hidden behind his lashes that were still spiked with moisture.

'I have something for you, too.'

It was the last thing she had expected him to say, and she bit her lip when he suddenly released her and strode over to his briefcase. He handed her a square, wrapped package, and she took it with a sinking heart. At least it felt too heavy to be more jewellery, she thought numbly, hoping that she could manage to sound suitably pleased with his gift, when inside her heart was breaking that he hadn't made any response, bar shock, when she had told him how she felt about him.

'Open it, *agape,*' he said quietly. 'I am not good with the words, and I've had so little practice in saying what I need to say. But my gift may explain better.'

Startled by the distinct tremor in his voice she fumbled with the packaging, and as she tore off the paper her heart—time, the universe—seemed to stand still. Even without her glasses she recognised the familiar book from her childhood, and suddenly her heart began to beat very fast.

'*Russian Fairy Tales and Fables*—the book my father used to read to me,' she whispered, her voice sounding as if it came from a long way off. 'I can't believe it. It's the most wonderful present you've ever given me, Nikos. Where on earth did you get it?' And, more importantly—why? she wanted to ask. But she was too afraid of his answer to voice the question.

'One of the reasons I went to New York was to meet the private collector who owned it, and persuade him to part with it.' Nikos stroked her hair back from her face with an unsteady hand, and the emotion that blazed in his eyes made her catch her breath.

'I know how much you miss your father, and how special this book is to you. I want—' he swallowed hard, emotion still clogging his throat

'—I want to be a good father to our child, Kitty. A father like you had—who reads stories every night and loves his child unreservedly.' He paused, and felt as though he were about to leap off a precipice, into the unknown. But then he looked into Kitty's soft brown eyes, saw the love there—her love for him—and he felt an arrow pierce his heart. 'But more important than that, I found the book because I didn't know how else to tell you that you are my life, Kitty, and all that I am, everything I have worked for, is meaning-less without you.'

Kitty took a ragged little breath, not daring to hope that he meant the words he had uttered in his velvet-soft tone. 'You don't have to pretend…or say things just because you think I want to hear them. I understand how your past must have affected you, and made it impossible for you to ever trust another person…'

Nikos placed his finger lightly across her lips. 'I trust you, Kitty *mou*,' he said, and with the words came an indescribable feeling of release and joy as he had never known before. His wife was honest and open, brave, and heartbreakingly generous. Her love for him shone in her eyes and he felt it wash over him and cleanse him until he felt weak with relief and empowered by the strength of *his* love for *her*.

'I love you, Kitty.' He drew her into his arms—

tentatively, as if she were made of finest porcelain and he was afraid she would break—and held her against his chest, feeling their hearts beat in unison. 'I think I probably fell in love with you when I mistook you for a waitress at the palace ball—and, certainly, after I had made love to you in the cave and you then disappeared. I tried everything to find you and if I had I would have hoped to have had a relationship with you.'

'You mean you were going to ask Rina to be your mistress?' Kitty queried, her eyes widening at his tender smile.

'It was all I could have offered, then,' he said, his voice low and aching with regret for the time he had wasted. 'I had vowed never to marry again, and certainly never to fall in love. But then I learned that there was a baby…and within weeks I had broken my first vow, and was fast on my way to breaking the second.'

'Oh, Nikos.' The expression in his eyes told her louder than any words that it was true—unbelievably, miraculously, he loved her. And because she understood how hard it must have been for him to admit his feelings to himself, let alone to her—and allow himself to be vulnerable and open to hurt—she loved him even more. Suddenly words were not enough, and she reached up to cup his face with her hands and brushed her mouth over his, emotion flooding through her when he responded instantly and kissed her with such sweet passion, such *love*, that tears slipped silently down her cheeks.

'Don't cry,' he pleaded as he lifted her and carried her down the hall. 'I never want to make you cry, Kitty *mou*.' But his eyes were wet too when he reached their bedroom and stood her by the bed while he drew down the zip of her gold dress and gently tugged the material until it fell in a shimmering pool at her feet.

'You are so beautiful, so soft and perfectly formed,' he whispered against her mouth as he removed the rest of her clothes, his, and drew her down onto the bed, covering her body with his own. 'After what happened with Greta and the baby I felt frozen inside,' he admitted rawly. 'And to be honest I was glad that nothing ever touched my emotions. I didn't want to care for anyone ever again, and I told myself I was happy dating dozens of women who meant nothing to me.

'I didn't want to marry you, and I certainly didn't expect to fall in love with you, but bit by bit you crept under my guard. You were so generous and giving, and although you had enjoyed a privileged upbringing you cared so much for others who have nothing. Sometimes I think you want to change the world,' he said softly, smiling down at her. 'You changed me, Kitty. You made me feel again, and you made me see that I was being a coward by denying how I felt about you, even though I was sure you could not love me when I had forced you to leave the home you loved, and your family. We will move back to Aristo if you want,' he offered. 'I want you to be happy, Kitty, and I realised during the week I was in the States that I don't care where I live as long as I am with you.'

She shook her head firmly. 'You belong in Athens, Nikos, and I belong with you. But I agree; it doesn't really matter where we are, as long as we're together—you, me, and soon the baby.' She traced her fingers over his jaw and the sensual curve of his mouth, and felt desire flood through her when his body stirred against hers. 'But, Nikos, do you think we could stop talking now?' she whispered against his mouth. 'So that I can show you how much I love you.'

And she did with such passion and generosity and the love that she no longer had to hide from him that Nikos's heart overflowed with the emotions he had denied for so long. And when he moved over her and joined them as one, it seemed to him that their souls as well as their bodies had fused, and he knew that the love they shared would last a lifetime.

THE ROYAL HOUSE OF KAREDES

Two crowns, two islands, one legacy

A royal family, torn apart by pride and its lust for power, reunited by purity and passion

The islands of Adamas have been torn into
two rival kingdoms:

TWO CROWNS
The Stefani diamond has been split as a
symbol of their feud

TWO ISLANDS
Gorgeous Greek princes reign supreme
over glamorous Aristo
Smouldering sheikhs rule the desert island of Calista

ONE LEGACY
Whoever reunites the diamonds will rule all.

Turn the page to discover more!

THE KINGDOM OF ADAMAS: A TURBULENT HISTORY

The islands of Calista and Aristo have always been a temptation to world powers. Initially this was because of their excellent positions for trading and the agricultural potential of Aristo's luscious, fertile land. The discovery of diamonds on Calista in the Middle Ages made the kingdom a target for invaders.

The kingdom passed through the hands of many foreign powers throughout the ages. Originally part of the Ancient Greek Empire, Adamas then came under the control of Rome from 150 BC onwards. Following the fall of the Roman Empire approximately four hundred years later, the islands were annexed to Byzantine control.

It was not until Richard the Lionheart seized Adamas in the twelfth century that the family of Karedes, local island nobility, was installed on the throne. When the republic of Venice briefly took control in the fifteenth century the Karedes dynasty continued to rule as mere figureheads.

Thereafter followed a period of struggle for the royal family. The Ottoman Empire claimed the islands in the sixteenth century and they were forced into an exile that lasted nearly two hundred years. When the Turks finally sold the islands to the British in 1750 the royal family was finally reinstated but the kingdom did not gain its independence until 1921.

The death of King Christos in 1974 marked the end of the kingdom of Adamas. The islands have functioned under separate rule ever since.

THE STEFANI DIAMOND

Diamonds have been prized since the dawn of human history for their unique qualities. The jewels were first discovered in India in 800 BC, and brought to Europe by Alexander the Great five hundred years later.

In 1477, Mary of Burgundy became the first known recipient of a diamond engagement ring given to her by the Archduke Maximilian of Austria. This begins the history and tradition of diamond engagement rings.

The Koh-i-Noor and the Hope diamonds were brought to Europe in 1631. In 1792, the Hope Diamond was stolen from the French crown jewels during the French Revolution. In 1851, The Koh-i-Noor diamond was re-cut to one hundred and five carats for Queen Victoria (Empress of India). This famous diamond is part of the British Crown jewels.

In the medieval period, a beautiful pink diamond was discovered on Calista, and used in the Karedes crown to symbolise the power of the Karedes's rule. The jewel became known as the Stefani (meaning: Crown) diamond. It quickly took on a deeply symbolic role in the kingdom of Adamas. Believing that their power resided in the stone, the Karedes family vowed that it would never leave their hands. If the jewel was lost, their kingdom would fall. The existence of this diamond fuelled treasure-hunters' dreams for centuries, but no other diamond of any size was found on Calista until the 1940s.

In 1972, faced with increasing tension from his kingdom, the islands of Aristo and Calista and with family pressure, King Christos announced that after his death the two islands would split. In the presence of his children Anya and Aegeus, witnessed by the court, Christos declared:

"You will rule each island for the good of the people, and bring out the best in your kingdom, but my wish is that eventually these two jewels, like the islands, will be reunited. Aristo and Calista are more successful, more beautiful and more powerful as one nation, Adamas."

After King Christos died in 1974, the one Stefani diamond was split into two, to form two stones for the coronation crowns of Aristo and Calista and fulfil the ancient charter.

THE TOURIST'S GUIDE TO ARISTO AND CALISTA

The island of Aristo

The island's name itself means best – and it certainly lives up to that as a holiday destination! The sunny climate and beautiful coastline have made it a favourite destination for jet-set holidaymakers. It is an incredibly rich principality, a world-renowned financial centre and provides tranquil luxury and a decadent party scene, complete with fabulous restaurants and nightclubs, a golf course, a marina and a casino.

Things to see

Don't miss the impressive Royal Palace in the centre of the island, just inland from the bay of Apollonia. The beautiful old quarter and port of Messaria are well worth a visit – especially to spend your casino winnings in fabulous boutiques! Long white sandy beaches on the north-east coast are banked by fertile plains. A number of fabulous tourist resorts are dotted along the north-east coast where the rich and famous can relax in five-star hotels and spas, or in gated mansions with infinity pools, private tennis courts and landscaped gardens. If your taste is more for city life, enjoy the ultra-modern city, Ellos, where high-rise corporations reach for the sky.

Things to do

Ellos is packed with exclusive bars, restaurants and spas and is famous for its glittering nightlife. The Grand Hotel is the centre of Ellos's nightlife – don't miss your chance to spot celebrities in its fabulous restaurant!

The island of Calista

Calista (meaning: beautiful one) is the destination of choice for more laid-back tourism. The sleepy island is an unspoiled paradise with an understated tourism industry. In contrast to neighbouring island Aristo, Calista has a hot, dry climate and arid terrain. The central portion of the island is entirely desert and inhabitants reside on the more hospitable north-facing coast. As its agricultural prospects have never been great, the island has retained its stunning natural beauty. Famous for the wealth of diamonds below the surface of the rock, the main river Kordela is also source of glittering diamond deposits.

Things to see

Modern Calista has an intact historical centre called Serapolis which is still the beating heart of the city. It retains a strong middle-eastern influence both culturally and architecturally and noisy, colourful markets fill the labyrinth of winding streets. Don't miss the beautiful Royal Palace.

Things to do

You'll pick up bargains and enjoy some delicious street food in the marketplace of Serapolis. Explore the Azahar desert – on the back of a camel for the intrepid – and spend a night in an oasis. Walk the diamond fields and try to find your own glittering stone as a souvenir of your stay in this peaceful place. For an injection of glamour and luxury, visit the new town and resort of Jaladhar.

LETTERS FROM
THE HOUSE OF KAREDES

A hastily scribbled note to Andonis, grounds keeper at the Royal Palace, from Princess Anya:

Andonis,

It is all over. I have lost our baby because of Aegeus. My brother discovered our affair and he was angry – so angry that he hit me. I fell and now our child is gone, Andonis. I cannot bear it. My brother has ruined everything. I will never forgive Aegeus for the hurt that he has caused, but our love is cursed. We cannot be together.

Anya

Aegeus to Lydia, his maid, in 1974 on the death of his father:

Dearest Lydia,

Love, you must put me from your mind. Forced by duty and by circumstance, I must go through with my betrothal. Tia deserves better than this, but my family and my loyalty demand this farce of a wedding.

It would be better if you were to go to Calista for now. I don't trust myself to remain near you and remember my duty. We must part. But come to me in Aristo every year on the anniversary of our wedding. It is not enough. It will never be enough. Wear the diamond for me.

I know you will understand, my beautiful Lydia. It is a son's duty and the king's command.

Yours eternally,

Aegeus

CHANTELLE SHAW

lives on the Kent coast, five minutes from the sea, and does much of her thinking about the characters in her books while walking on the beach. She's been an avid reader from an early age. Her schoolfriends used to hide their books when she visited – but Chantelle would retreat into her own world, and still writes stories in her head all the time. Chantelle has been blissfully married to her own tall, dark and very patient hero for over twenty years, and has six children. She began to read Mills & Boon® books as a teenager and, throughout the years of being a stay-at-home mum to her brood, found romantic fiction helped her to stay sane! She enjoys reading and writing about strong-willed, feisty women, and even stronger-willed sexy heroes. Chantelle is at her happiest when writing. She is particularly inspired while cooking dinner, which unfortunately results in a lot of culinary disasters! She also loves gardening, walking, and eating chocolate (followed by more walking!). Catch up with Chantelle's latest news on her website, www.chantelleshaw.com.

Read on for our exclusive interview with Chantelle Shaw!

We chatted to Chantelle Shaw about the world of THE ROYAL HOUSE OF KAREDES. Here are her insights!

Would you prefer to live on Aristo or Calista? What appeals to you most about either island?

I think I would prefer to live on Aristo – known as the jewel in the Mediterranean – because it has stunning scenery, fabulous beaches and fantastic shopping and nightlife. Who wouldn't want to live in a millionaire's paradise! But the wildness and beauty of the desert on Calista appeals to my romantic nature.

What did you enjoy about writing about The Royal House of Karedes?

I liked the fact that the stories and characters in the Royal House of Karedes are all interwoven, and yet at the same time I was given the opportunity to make the storyline I was given my own. The locations and the fact that the stories were set around a royal dynasty meant lots of Presents glamour which was great fun to write!

How did you find writing as part of a continuity?

It was the first time I have written a continuity book, and rather daunting when some of the other authors are so much more experienced than me. But it was a great honour, and I enjoyed taking part. I can't wait to read all the other books in the series.

When you are writing, what is your typical day?

On a typical day I write from 9.30am until 3.00pm while my children are at school. In the evening, after sorting out dinner, homework and after-school clubs, I often write for another hour or so, and I try to snatch some time at weekends, especially as my story develops and I want to know what will happen next.

Where do you get your inspiration for the characters that you write?

Inspiration for my characters is difficult to explain. They usually just come into my head and I know exactly what they look like – hair colour etc, and usually they arrive with a name, but sometimes I look through a name book and one will jump out that I know instinctively is right for my character. I think about the character's background right back to childhood and I make loads of notes that I don't often use in the book but help me to really know the person I am writing about. I also spend quite a lot of time thinking and researching the character's job, interests and talents.

What did you like most about your hero and heroine in this continuity?

I liked my heroine, Kitty, because she seemed a very real person, and like many of us she was insecure about her body and how she looked. Her lack of confidence made being in the public eye an ordeal for her, but despite her shyness she forced herself to carry out her royal duties. Her gentle demeanour hid a strong will and she also had a deeply compassionate nature. My hero, Nikos, seemed like a ruthless businessman and a playboy, but underneath his vulnerability made me like him. He had developed a tough shell because he had been hurt by so many things in his past. Not knowing the identity of his father troubled him and made him feel as if he was only half a person – and later he had been devastated when he was cruelly betrayed by his first wife who he had loved.

What would be the best – and worst – things about being part of a royal dynasty?

The best thing about being part of a royal dynasty would be the glamorous lifestyle and the opportunities for travel. The worst would be constantly being in the public eye with your every move scrutinised by the media (Prince William and Kate Middleton spring to mind).

Are diamonds really a girl's best friend?

Are diamonds a girl's best friend? Well – I have been married to my lovely husband for twenty-six years – and I've never owned a diamond. When we got engaged all those years ago he couldn't afford an expensive engagement ring. Something sparkly would be nice – but he is definitely my best friend, and for me love is more important than "things".

*Who will reunite the Stefani Diamond
and rule Adamas?*

Don't miss the next book in the fabulous
ROYAL HOUSE OF KAREDES:

THE FUTURE KING'S LOVE-CHILD

BY MELANIE MILBURNE

The prince's baby of shame

Cassie Kyriakis was wrongly accused of murdering
her father and *jailed*, leaving her wild-child roots and
Seb, her one true love, behind her…

Now the throne awaits Prince Sebastian Karedes!

Seb had once loved Cassie so passionately he would
have chosen her over his kingdom. But she rejected
him. Now she's been released from prison, he
discovers that she may be innocent of her crime – but
she gave birth to his baby in her cell! Sebastian must
choose between his own honour and his duty to his
kingdom. He will claim his love-child – but what
about his bride?

Turn the page for
an exclusive extract!

Cassie was just congratulating herself on getting through two hours of successfully shielding herself behind the Aristo palace's pillars and pot plants, dodging both the press and Prince Regent Sebastian Karedes, when she suddenly came face to face with him.

She swallowed thickly, her heart coming to a clunking stop in her chest as her eyes went to his inscrutable dark brown ones so far above hers. She opened her mouth to speak but her throat was too tight to get a single word out. She felt the slow creep of colour staining her cheeks, and wondered if he had any idea of how much over the last six years she had dreaded this moment.

"Cassie." His deep voice was like a warm velvet glove stroking along the bare skin of her shivering arms. "Have you only just arrived? I had not seen you until a few moments ago."

Cassie moistened her dry-as-parchment lips with the tip of her tongue. "Um…no," she said shifting her gaze sideways. "I've been here all evening…"

A small silence began to weight the

atmosphere, like humidity just before a storm.

"I see."

Cassie marvelled at how he could inject so much into saying so little. Those two little words contained disdain and distrust, and something else she couldn't quite put her finger on.

"So why are you here?" he asked, his eyes narrowing even further. "I do not recall seeing your name on the official guest list."

Cassie swept the point of her tongue across her lips again, trying to keep her gaze averted. "As part of my...um...parole programme I took a job at the orphanage," she said, loathing the shame she could feel staining her face. "I've been working there for the last eleven months."

When he didn't respond immediately Cassie felt compelled to bring her gaze back to his but then wished she hadn't.

A corner of his mouth was lifted in an unmistakably mocking manner. "*You* are looking after children?"

She felt herself bristling. "Yes," she clipped out. "I enjoy every minute of it. I'm here tonight with some of the other carers and educational staff. They insisted I attend."

Another tight silence began to shred at Cassie's nerves. She would have given just about anything to have avoided coming here this evening. She had felt as if she had been playing a high-stakes game of hide-and-seek all night, the strain of keeping out of the line of Sebastian's deep brown gaze had made her head pound with sickening tension. Even now the hammer blows behind her eyes were making it harder and harder for her to keep her manner cool and unaffected before him.

His commanding and totally charismatic presence both drew her and terrified her, but the very last thing she wanted was for him to realise it.

She surreptitiously fondled the smooth pearls of the bracelet around her wrist, the only thing she still had left of her mother's, hoping it would give her the courage and fortitude to get through the next few minutes until she could make good her escape.

"Well then," he said, as his eyes continued to skewer hers, that sardonic half-smile still in place, "as the royal patron of the orphanage you now work for, I would have thought you would have made every effort to include yourself in this evening's proceedings rather than hide behind the flower arrangements."

Cassie's chin came up. "And have the press hound me for an exclusive photo and interview?" she asked. "Not until my parole is up. Maybe then I'll think about it."

His eyes began to burn with brooding intensity. "I must say I am surprised you haven't already sold your story to the press, Cassie," he said. "But perhaps I should warn you before you think about doing so. One word about our…" he paused over the word for an infinitesimal pause, "past involvement and I will have you thrown back into prison where the majority of the population of Aristo believes you still belong. Have I made myself clear?"

THE ROYAL HOUSE OF KAREDES

Two crowns, two islands, one legacy

Volume Eight
THE DESERT KING'S HOUSEKEEPER BRIDE
by Carol Marinelli

Claimed by the sheikh – for her innocence!

Housekeeper Effie, a practical, slightly dumpy virgin, has been summoned to the desert to serve ruthless Sheikh King Zakari.

After hot, amazing hours of passion, Effie's heart is near to bursting. But what she doesn't realise is that something will compel Zakari to take her, a lowly servant, as his royal bride!

Available 20th November 2009

THE ROYAL HOUSE OF KAREDES

Two crowns, two islands, one legacy

Volume 1 – April 2009
BILLIONAIRE PRINCE, PREGNANT MISTRESS
by Sandra Marton

Volume 2 – May 2009
THE SHEIKH'S VIRGIN STABLE-GIRL
by Sharon Kendrick

Volume 3 – June 2009
THE PRINCE'S CAPTIVE WIFE
by Marion Lennox

Volume 4 – July 2009
THE SHEIKH'S FORBIDDEN VIRGIN
by Kate Hewitt

8 VOLUMES IN ALL TO COLLECT!

THE ROYAL HOUSE OF KAREDES

Two crowns, two islands, one legacy

8 VOLUMES IN ALL TO COLLECT!

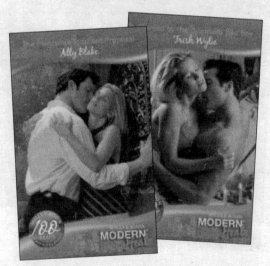